I0736152

PRONATOR

James A. Landry

Pronator

This book is written to provide information and motivation to readers. Its purpose is not to render any type of psychological, legal, or professional advice of any kind. The content is the sole opinion and expression of the author, and not necessarily that of the publisher.

Copyright © 2020 by James A. Landry

All rights reserved. No part of this book may be reproduced, transmitted, or distributed in any form by any means, including, but not limited to, recording, photocopying, or taking screenshots of parts of the book, without prior written permission from the author or the publisher. Brief quotations for noncommercial purposes, such as book reviews, permitted by Fair Use of the U.S. Copyright Law, are allowed without written permissions, as long as such quotations do not cause damage to the book's commercial value. For permissions, write to the publisher, whose address is stated below.

Printed in the United States of America.

ISBN   978-1-951913-07-6   (Paperback)
ISBN   978-1-951913-08-3   (Digital)

Lettra Press books may be ordered through booksellers or by contacting:

Lettra Press LLC
30 N Gould St. Suite 4753
Sheridan, WY 82801, USA
1 307-200-3414 | info@lettrapress.com
www.lettrapress.com

Dedications

My Incredible Dad

Norman R. Landry (R.I.P.)

Also, to my man in The Show

My Godfather

Jimmy Piersall (R.I.P.)

STORY AND WRITING REVIEWS

". . .J.A. Landry has a writing style that puts you right into the scene and gets right under the skin of his characters."

". . .when I bought the book, I began reading it right away. Simply stated, I could not put it down, and I finished it within two days. J.A. Landry spins a dynamite adult fiction tale, his writing style puts the reader right into the story, and the characterizations and dialog are just right."

". . .As I read. . . my emotions ran a surprisingly broad gamut in response to the lives and actions that Landry spun together; it is a ride. . . that is at once believable, frightening in its implications and entertaining. This is a book I will read a second time."

". . .His story is a ride worth hanging on for as Landry twirls his readers through the psychotic tour of a bohemian rock and roll star."

". . .I couldn't put this book down! All my questions were answered! The ending was excellent. When the ride is over you are left wanting more! I can't wait to read another J.A. Landry book!"

OTHER FINE BOOKS BY JAMES A. LANDRY

"Pronator"

"Fool Star"

"Solitary Refinement"

"Above Beyond"

"Eaves Drop"

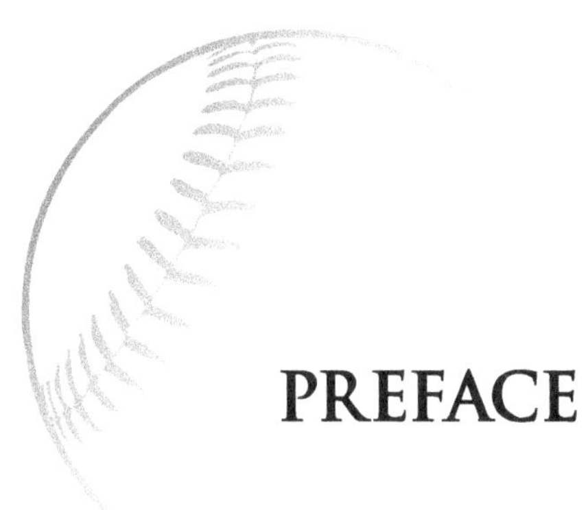

PREFACE

Sample of Baseball Pitches

Slider

An underrated pitch that every hurler should have in his arsenal. When you get a pitcher that gives it good movement and good location, it's untouchable.

Knuckle-Curve

No one believes you when you say you throw one, but it's like a Curveball on steroids. The index finger creates more spin than a regular Curveball, providing an even more dominant Curveball, thus more strikeouts. It confuses the batter perspective.

Fastball

It better have good location and be really fast. All Coaches pick this pitch.

Four-Seam Fastball

Younger players base their pitches on this specific pitch. The hell is this. . . when someone pitches you a Fastball, it's a dinger: The ball doesn't move on the batter.

Two-Seam Fastball

This is the 2nd fastest pitch in the game, *and* it moves on the hitter, therefore making it the preferred Fastball to many Pitchers and Catchers.

Three-Seam Fastball

A top five pitch. Slightly off-speed from the Two-Seamer.

Curveball

Virtually every pitcher, college-level pitcher and up, must have a Curveball, or better yet, an array of them. The ball moves bigtime on the batter.

Split-Finger Fastball (Splitter)

Splitters are great pitches because they don't damage-up your arm like Curves and Sliders are prone to. With the proper location they break enough to get any batter out.

Gyroball

This can be a truly magic pitch: It gets in a batter's head. The batter thinks he sees it rising when it's dropping. It's an entirely awesome pitch, yet a rarely seen gem.

Screwball

When used, this can be the best pitch in the game. It's not easy to learn or throw but nearly impossible to hit.

Knuckle Ball

It's a tricky pitch, although it's prone to be hit for homers if left up high in the strike zone but otherwise a very hard to hit, well-rounded pitch. Wind against a pitcher or no wind at all makes the Knuckle Ball move, loop and jump even more. It will break three or four times at the least before reaching the plate. The ball basically has a mind of its own; like 'cork kernel brain.'

Sinker

There are still some pitchers that make this their most feared pitch of the game. The ball drops approaching the batter.

Cutter

It perplexes baseball people everywhere that this isn't the number one pitch. Mariano Rivera revolutionized it. Then, pitchers, year by year, find out the wonders of this pitch. You think it is a Fastball, then it breaks hard and away. It tricks the hitter looking like a Fastball but then -- *doink* -- it moves. The cut Fastball grip is half Four-Seamer, plus half Slider.

Spitball

This pitch uses moisture to alter the shape of the ball, making it into an oblong and virtually impossible to hit. This pitch is so nasty that it is banned from the league. But still, some pitchers and catchers try to execute it, just hoping they don't get caught. And there are many ingenious methods to render it.

Eephus Pitch or Playball

This pitch dramatically drops on the batter and looks like a clown pitch, best used on heavy hitters. It can be thrown in the 40s. It really does confuse hitters, floating in but then drops straight down as it reaches the plate.

Curveball (Over-Arcing)

Many throw this one: It's wicked hard to get a bat on it, and it is easy to learn, too. This is usually the first outright traditional Curveball learned by most young pitchers.

Meatball

It is the middle of April, and the score is tied between the Miami Marlins and Seattle Mariners. It is the bottom of the 9th inning, the bases are loaded, and nobody is out. Marlins masher Giancarlo Stanton is at the plate against Mariners reliever Yoervis Medina, and Medina is ahead one ball and two strikes, in position to put Stanton away and extend the inning. But then he makes a terrible mistake with a breaking ball, hanging it high, and Stanton knows what to do with this mistake. The pitch is a "meatball;" a pitch so appetizing a hitter can't help but think of devouring it whole. And big-league batters can eat. They don't leave many meatballs on the plate.

Foshball

What a great pitch. It's very much like a Splitter but with some tail away from a right-handed batter. There are technically two ways to grip it as well, both resulting in the same movement but with different speed. The Fosh, Foshball, or Fosh Change is a seldom used pitch in Major League Baseball, described as 'a cross between a Split-Fingered pitch and a straight Change-Up.'

It is designed to fool a batter expecting a Fastball to have to contend with a slower pitch. The pitch has a grip like a Fastball, but the index and middle fingers are spread slightly across the baseball, and the ring and little finger wrap around the side of the ball. If thrown properly, it has characteristics like a breaking Change-up or an off-speed Split-Finger Fastball. The origin of the Fosh is unknown, although Mike Boddicker was the first pitcher known to throw it. It's a noxiously good pitch but very underrated, and rarely seen.

Vulcan Change-up

The pitch (otherwise known as a Vulcan or Trekkie) is a type of Change-up; it closely resembles a Forkball and Split-Finger Fastball. It is a variation of the circle Change-up, and when mastered can be extremely effective. Much like a Forkball, the Vulcan is gripped between two fingers on the hand but rather than the middle and index finger as with the Forkball or Split-Finger Fastball, it sits in between the middle and ring fingers to make a V-shape (Vulcan salute) when releasing to the catcher. It is thrown with Fastball arm speed but by pronating the hand by turning the thumb down, to get good downward movement on it.

Circle Change-up

This is a pitch thrown with a grip that includes a circle formation, like the Palm Ball Change-up, hence the name. The circle is formed by making a circle with the index finger, holding the thumb at the bottom of the ball parallel to the middle finger and holding the ball far out in the hand. The ball is thrown pronating the forearm, turning the palm out.

Both those Change-ups are amazing pitches; crosses between a Change-up and a Sinker.

<u>The Bean Ball</u>.

When a Fastball goes by a batter with high velocity – 'velo,' it looks like the size of a pea. A plate-crowding batter is a prime target for a Bean Ball. Even though he's seldom hit, he backs up and off the plate after the threatening warning from the plate-owning pitcher.

THE
COSTELLO
FAMILY

1

Art Costello is under heavy sedation for pain as the doctors in the VA Dispensary at the Portsmouth Naval Shipyard prepare him for surgery. Cruising too close to the North Korean waters on the USS Dupont, he catches a heavy cap of shrapnel that runs through the back of his neck and rips across his shoulders.

He reports back to the Portsmouth Naval Shipyard on the USS Dupont following his deployments during WWII and the Korean Conflict. It's familiar territory to the

Chief Officer. He just wants some white tees, skivvies, denim shirts and comfortable jeans.

Once out of bed but while healing at the shipyard, he is assigned light submarine inspection detail. While he is an inspector for this leg of his service, he meets a young lady from Eagle Lake, Maine. She is a 19-year-old Lead Arc Welder. He gets a kick out of that, not in a chauvinistic way but with a raised respect for her, thus spawning more affection between both like they have not felt before.

Sophia is the most beautiful and sweetest woman Art has ever met. She mutually shares those feelings for him, too. They volunteer for the USO together. They do a lot of things together, going into Portsmouth and other surrounding destinations. When the days are done, or they are off, weekends or otherwise, they head out to the White Mountains, Rye Beach, Hampton or Boston.

Sophia's Eagle Lake is way up north there in Aroostook County. Art hunts and fishes in the county but not as far north as Eagle Lake, which is only 12 miles from Fort Kent.

The Fort Kent -- Clair Border Crossing is at the Clair-Fort Kent Bridge that connects the town of Fort Kent, Maine, with Clair, New Brunswick, on the Canada-United States border. It marks the Northern Terminus of U.S. Route 1. The Southern Terminus is in Key West, Florida.

Sophia speaks little English, and Art speaks no French at all but that doesn't stop them from courting immediately and set out to teach each other their native dialects. It's impossible to lose any patience with her: She is just that alluring and pleasant. She is a quicker study than he is. He manages to hold in his frustration only by Sophia's fine nature and sense of humor.

Since most of Art's family lives in or near Portsmouth, presenting Sophia to them is easy, and she is immediately accepted and adored. Being so charming with her cute French accent and her working on her own make her even more charismatic and appealing.

Her family welcomes Art like he is a long-missing family member. The population of Eagle Lake is 241 and it seems that Sophia is somehow related to all of them! She and Art go from house to house, eating dessert before dinner, then more after supper with coffee. It's a French thing.

Art makes several new hunting and fishing buddies. The men are big, strong and tough, and most work in the woods, sometimes weeks at a time, while the women take care over their homes and children. They may also join their husbands to assist in camp clean-up, supper and dinner.

Nephew Larry comes back from Germany terminally disabled after an accident; runover by a Unimog. He arrives back home along with the very nurse who cared for him overseas. She is originally from Pennsylvania but is so much more an upper Maine girl. Thankfully, she knows enough French that she is Art's stand-by translator when needed; when Sophia or another relative is not close by.

Art hears the stories of Sophia riding to school, friends in tow, on her father's horse and sleigh. The buggy is also useful, but the ground is frozen and snow-covered eight or nine months out of twelve.

Art also learns of Sophia's brush with death after she is hit by a drunken driver. She is 16 and gathered with friends on the corner of Route 11-Main Street and 2nd

Street in midafternoon, when a drunken out-of-towner in a 1940 Ford Deluxe Convertible Club Coupe came out of nowhere and mowed Sophia down. The passenger side wheels took her midsection and the driver's side broke her two legs just below the knee.

The Costellos marry in Art's hometown in New Hampshire after 16 months of courtship. He makes sure that all of Sophia's family and friends who wish to attend have the transportation to get there. Trips out of town almost never take place in Eagle Lake; and to know the land and its people, it's easy to see why not.

The ceremony is an informal and laidback affair. Not just because that's Art's and Sophia's taste -- which is comfort -- but he does not want the Eagle Lakers to feel they need to purchase new clothes just to attend.

Sophia acknowledges that "this is just the way he is."

Art buys a small home in Panaway Manor, which is an early 1940s development built mainly for off-base housing supporting Pease Air Base in Portsmouth. Sophia and Art enjoy having some time to spare, to relax after being on the go for so long. Moods remain high like an extended honeymoon, and they enjoy meeting all their new neighbors and unpacking their goods.

In a welcome surprise, within three months of moving in, Sophia and Art learn she is pregnant. After all, they were not trying *not* to conceive. Daughter Tristy comes along soon afterward, followed by another daughter, Anita, 14 months later.

From day one, the little girls behave like mortal enemies. It's not something they pick up at home. Art and Sophia are loving and close, not just to each other but to both daughters, as well.

Mom and Dad are notified by the OB/GYN that Sophia suffers an inverted uterus after birthing Anita, and unfortunately could never become pregnant again. Dad is especially downhearted, because as much as he loves his girls, he, like most men, deeply wishes for a son.

He and Sophia continue to pray to God. It's bad enough that his girls torture him so, but there are so many things he looks forward to teaching his boy, should God have mercy.

The young parents aggrieve twofold. First, growing up, their two daughters are constantly at each other's throats, and the tension drives Dad crazy. They fight over clothes, jewelry, boys, television shows, the car, money, friends, seniority, privacy infringements, copying one another and who gets to sit in the front seat of the car.

"Ugh! The party never ends." Art often scoffs.

He is happily surprised when he is finally awarded his Honorable Discharge along with other medals for bravery and valor. This means he can rent that apartment in Manhattan's Lower East Side and finally get a lot of work that has been left hanging, done. He's been setting-up gigs and conducting business remote from New England for too long. He announces it at dinner, and Sophia and their two daughters are genuinely excited by the chance to visit 'The Big City.'

Sophia is enamored, and star struck at all the celebrities Art knows and works with;

multitudes of professional sports figures; movie stars, Bob Hope; the Rat Pack; Joey Heatherton; Barbara Eden; Sid Caesar; Bob Parkinson and his picture-perfect wife, Miss Universe, Barbara Parkinson; Allan King; Rocky Marciano; Ed Sullivan, Bob Keechan (Captain Kangaroo); Norm Crosby; Hugh Hefner; and so many more, including Beatles promoter Sid Bernstein and manager Brian Epstein.

Art even procures tickets for The Beatles Atlantic City show for Tristy and Anita. It is understandable. He is a Promoter, Ad Man and Public Relations man, too.

Art becomes, in time, the Rockingham County Commissioner, a high-ranking officer of the Port Authority, and holds other posts throughout New Hampshire, Massachusetts and Maine. He owns one third of the Miss Universe Pageant franchise. He raises the incomparable

Osbourne-Kemper-Thomas Ad Agency from the ground up to the top of the heap.

He is the Portsmouth Recreation Director and the publisher of "The Beacon" periodical for the Portsmouth Chamber of Commerce. He founded Jubilee Week in Portsmouth. It is Portsmouth's answer to Mardi Gras -- a week-long celebration chockfull of events, entertainment and fun all over town.

While in New York, he shoots a series of television advertisements for the new Speidel Twist-O-Flex watches. He's popular on television. People recognize him, which just tickles Sophia. That, in turn, makes his kids feel like mini-celebrities.

Art is one very busy man, yet to ask him, he'd say, "It's a *good* kind of busy. You know?"

2

The smell hits him the second he steps out
of the elevator. He enters the apartment and
steps back as if being smacked in the face
with a smelly, old, damp washcloth. He walks
slowly through the home, following his nose
like a bloodhound. He knows Mom took Tristy
shopping for a new blouse at the PX.

He doesn't think about it or know why he
is creeping around; instinct, perhaps. The
stench is foreign to the Costello home, but
he knows all too well what it is. He slides
open Anita's closet door so fiercely that the
door rails above break loose. And there she

is. . .sitting in there. . .smoking a fucking cigarette!

"Anita!" Dad yells and rips both sliding doors off the tracks to the floor. He knows what she is doing, but in the moment, he wails.

"What the heck do you think you're doing?"

"Smoking a cigarette."

"Yeah. You're so damn intelligent!" In a cartoon character voice, he mocks her.

"*Smoking a cigarette.*"

"Like smoking in your bedroom closet is going to hide in secrecy that rank stink? Seriously Anita? Am I looking at idiocy? I want to punish you for smoking to begin with, but I'm also going to punish you for being so gwad-dam *stupid* along with it!

"Now, you wash every stitch of fabric from

your closet, your bedroom dresser, Tristy's closeted clothes, *and* everything from her dresser, too!

"Now get to it! And don't forget the curtains and linen, either."

Art is an ex-smoker -- two packs a day -- but the very morning the cancer scare is announced over the car radio, he takes two cartons of Winstons he just bought out of the brown bag and tosses them out of the car window. That is the one and only time he ever littered. And, he never touched another smoke in his life.

He gains 20 pounds but likes himself better a chubby nonsmoker than an addicted, poisoned, more narrow-looking guy. . .with a cigarette butt hanging out of his lips.

"Tristy! Tristy!" Art bounds around the Cross-Beach Motel at the corner of Marylin Road. It is right across from the boardwalk and beach. Young people set asunder and scatter everywhere, but not Tristy.

"Tristy, I know you're here, you. . .you get yourself over here *now! Please.*"

The older of his two daughters comes to her father's side, shivering, and by the looks of the others there, covered only with a beach towel. The skinny-dipping pool party was planned weeks ago when the owner's son learned he'd be home alone for a weekend.

"Another intown genius." Art mutters.

Dads know all. Incidents in low places went on with the teen girls one after another, if not his girls, their best friends. Art realizes he's not the only one constantly on the lookout. He pinpoints.

Based on the lyrics, he disallows the girls to listen to certain songs, like "Under the Boardwalk."

"We'll be makin' love. . .Under the boardwalk. . ."

And of course, many others of the times, like the infamous lyricist Gary Puckett with The Union Gap.

"Young girl get out of my mind..."

Mom keeps the home quiet as she can and keeps good meals on the table, as Dad's role includes doling out the discipline. If his lucky silver Kennedy coin doesn't bounce off the tight hospital-cornered bedspreads, he tosses all the bedclothes out the window where they land in a cotton heap seven floors below.

Art's work is done for now in NYC, so the family works on packing up. A small moving van and a couple of men assist in the relocation. The family is glad to be home, though they all see more New York City visits coming in the future.

All his brothers have boys, and girls but unfortunately, they all live under the chronic mood changer-exchanger, alcohol and mean tempers. Most all the children, cousins, consider Uncle Art their father.

As the girls grow older into full-fledged preteens, and their troublesome ways only worsen, dreams of a good boy soothe, no matter what the doctor said, breaking the dismal news after Anita's birth.

The teens fight on high heels and wear boxing gloves. They fight about everything, anything. Who wore the other's sweater? Who deserves the local hunk all the girls want? Whose turn is it to do the dishes?

Art decides they've outgrown their home in Panaway Manor, so reaching for more space after moving back to Portsmouth, he buys a 44-acre parcel cornered at Banfield and Ocean Roads.

He develops a newer suburbia by dividing out and selling oversized lots along both avenues. Costello's home is a 250-year-old fieldstone hunting lodge crowned atop a moderate elevation of earth and ledge. The home's stone walls are three feet thick. It is the highest point in Portsmouth. Everyone in the family have their own room, and Art has an office.

The relocation does improve the girls' temperament, at least some. Maybe it will get better and better as time goes on. But, many of those seemingly accidents were nothing less than seeds quickly sprouting violent breakouts.

Chasing each other, Tristy pushes Anita through the porch storm door. Anita shrieks as the glass shatters and causes her to fall through. It is ugly, bloody and is painful. If blood holds any bearing, it hurts more than anyone else could know.

Tristy somehow becomes spoiled and narcissistic, and the younger of the two has been holding a deep, dark secret for going on two years. It nearly brings her down, she is almost always depressed, but she does her best to keep quiet and live through it. She does well in school.

Dad is the only child of sixteen who escapes alcoholism. He is a straight-up man. A hard-working man. A great man. One by one, his brothers and sisters each drop dead of alcohol-abuse-related diseases, such as liver poisoning, cirrhosis of the liver and hepatitis-C.

3

"Mrs. Costello! I have some news for you. It's certainly a surprise to me." The doctor has a hard time squelching a smile.

"Well, OK. Out with it, please. Am I ill?"

"Remember seven years ago, I said you'd never be able to become pregnant again because of your inverted uterus?"

"Yes, of course."

"Mrs. Costello, your uterus has corrected itself. . .it kind of flip-flopped."

"So, this means I stand a chance of birthing another child? Really?"

"Yes. Indeed."

The Missus jumps up, hugs the doctor, and cries something in French.

"Mrs. Costello, you are already pregnant. Mme. Costello, tu es déjà enceinte."

"Oh, mon Dieu," she begins in French. "My husband will be elated! Do we know the gender?"

"You should both decide if you'd really like to know that or not. Fair enough?"

"Ah, oui! Yes doctor," Mrs. Costello smiles through her tears as she steps out the door.

The sisters are ripping a mohair sweater apart in a fight over who's going to wear it. It is obvious to Mom and Dad that neither will, and he raises his voice.

"Just look at it! You've already practically shredded it!"

How they managed to ever share a bedroom is beyond all explanation. Dad walks through the archway into the wind of screams. He grabs each girl by the arm and announces that *nobody* will be going out tonight.

He marches back to the table.

"Um. . .Art," Sophia begins, a little over a whisper.

"Yes, doll."

"I went for my OB/GYN checkup today."

She whimpers, tears falling down her cheeks.

"Honey," she continues. "My uterus has, how he says, flipped de flopped."

"You mean it has reversed itself. It is no longer inverted?

"Yes."

"Really? Are you kidding me? Wow!" Art jumps up to hug her, and with his face nuzzled into her neck, she says, "Art, there is more."

"What is it? What is it Sophia, are you OK?"

"Art, my dear. I am pregnant." Tears sheet down her face.

He runs for a small towel.

"Wait. Are you happy about it?" He asks.

"Of course, I am!" Sophia bursts. "And I pray God delivers a precious boy for you. Us. . ."

"This is amazing, Sophia!"

"Art, the doctor said he could divulge the gender if we so wish. What do you think of that?"

"I fully admit, Sophie, I would like to

know. Of course, we both know we'd like a boy. He'll straighten those girls out!"

They both laugh softly, and then snicker at the thought.

Sophia books an appointment for the ultrasound; the experience she shares with her husband. They can hardly hide their eagerness the week and a half wait for it.

"At first, we wanted a surprise, but now our excitement is too much to bear. Art wants a boy so badly. If it's not, she'll be loved just the same, but he clearly wants that boy. Can you blame him, doctor?"

"Not at all!" The doctor says as he sets up the equipment.

"Most men want boys at any cost. You guys

have two girls, so I think a boy is quite in order." He chuckles. "Are you two ready?"

"Sure thing, doctor." Art says, even though the question was directed to his wife.

"OK Mrs. Costello, this ointment will feel chilly at first but not for long. Relax."

"Oh, do not worry about me," she laughs. "Keep your eye on *him*!" She nods toward Art. The more excited she is, the thicker her French accent comes through. It's very cute.

The doctor works on zeroing in on the itty-bitty baby in mommy's womb. The couple's patience feels tried. It seems so much longer than it looks on the shows and movies they've seen.

"Ah-ha!" The doctor has hit the target. "Can you both see from your angles?

"I think so." They answer in unison.

"OK folks, look close. . .right. . .*here*," the doctor says, designating a spot with an ultra-slim pocket round-tipped pointer. With a smile and a laugh, he says, "He's giving you a clear shot of his stuff!"

"Sophia, baby, look at that! it's a boy!"

"Oui! Yes, Art, we have a petite garcon; a little baby boy!"

As they hug, Art and Sophia cry openly, unabashedly.

"Well, now you have an idea of what colors to paint his nursery," the doctor suggests, "Not to mention his wardrobe." He laughs.

Then, the Costello's happy tears slowly turn to laughter, too.

As if ready to jump high through a ring

of fire, the baby boy is breech -- feet first -- and moving much too fast to afford correction. The Physician's Assistant tries to keep the pain at bay with mild injections encircling Sophia's vagina. Word has it that the doctor is presently on his way.

The Physician's Assistant asks Sophia to try to relax as she performs an episiotomy, a necessary procedure in her condition. Just after another shot, the PA snips a half-inch incision through the perineum, the skin from the vagina to the anus. This is better than the inevitable tearing that would otherwise occur. Sophia tenses and yelps, but it is over in a couple seconds.

The doctor arrives just in time to see two tiny feet seemingly struggling to get ground. He asks for space as he attempts to extract the boy without strangling him with the umbilical cord. Just as he does, the infant all but jumps into the doctor's hands out of his warm canal.

The doctor says loudly, "Well now! He is wide awake, loud and quite active for a nine-month plus two-minute-old *baby boy*!"

It's immediately time to perform two additional things (among many more to come). The Apgar score: Medline Plus must be done to a "T." In rare cases, the test will be done 10 minutes after birth. If the body is pink and the extremities are blue, the infant scores 1 for color. A score of 7, 8, or 9 is normal and is a sign that the newborn is in good health.

The Maternity Nurse announces, "All the fingers and toes made the journey. He is 19 ½ inches in height and weighs a healthy 6.5 pounds."

Finally, for the doctor today, it's time to collect the placenta. It falls straight into the large stainless-steel bowl with a deep squashy wet sound. It looks like a red, bloody octopus. Art almost throws up at the sight.

Sophia's doctor congratulates the Costellos for their patience and wherewithal in a truly shaky and scary incident. He gives a smile, a hug and a handshake just before their snapshot of him holding their newborn. On his way out, he thanks his PA for an impeccable job performed in his absence.

The following day is set for the circumcision, but Mom and baby will be home two days later. Tristy protests her father and mother for putting the infant boy through a circumcision. She will not give it up. She won't shut her big mouth. She fancies herself a female shaman of some sort and pretends to be some old wise woman who knows all there is to know.

"Hey, *Rhiannon*. . ." Art has had enough. He breaks his own Cardinal sin by cursing. "Shut the fuck up. And I mean shut up now or get the hell out of here and go home."

"Wait! Who? Who's Rhiannon?" Tristy excitedly asks.

"She rings like a bell through the night and wouldn't you love to love her?

"She rules her life like a bird in flight and who will be her lover?

"There! If you were of this world, you'd know that!"

It works well. Everybody within hearing range are cracking up.

Plans for Sammy's Baptism to celebrate the Christian infant--a guaranteed ticket into Heaven--are booked within 90 days. Art manages to bring in an old pal, the great Sam McDowell, for the role of Godfather. His wife is there, too. The Costellos name their son after McDowell.

Sam McDowell is an All-Star pitcher for the Cleveland Indians that Art met in the mid-sixties. The baby boy is named Samuel Edward Thomas Costello. Art and Sophia put up a grand party at home, while McDowell signs a ton of autographs and repeats something he will have said many times over to his namesake, "Kid. . .I am going to teach you how to play some ball!"

RAISING
THE GAME

4

Little Sammy's bedroom is completely decked out in all-things-baseball; from the bedspread and sheets, the throw rugs, area rugs, to the curtains and the various and ever-growing collection of baseball tchotchke.

He has several mitts and bats. There are miniature bats and plenty of hardballs, most of all his baseballs are autographed by the best of the best in Baseball through the 1950s and '60s.

Sammy learns early on about mitt design: Every design has a logical reasoning behind each stitch, depending on the position of the defensive fielders that wear them. The smaller pocketed gloves are for the infield players who must grab the ball out of the pocket quickly as possible to get the out; force out to any base or the plate, or to first base, or even score a double play.

The one exception is the first baseman's glove. It is fashioned as a long flat scoop like a large platypus bill. First base players get a lot of hasty throws in the dirt and must stretch to the max to capture the throw before the baserunner's foot reaches the bag, most called bang-bang plays because they are so close to call.

The larger bushel basket gloves serve an advantage to the outfielders, who must catch up with the hit, high in the air and snag it. Hence, the odd-looking and long woven cradle that is the crucial part of the mitt.

Often, the player must run, jump and reach

the arm all the way over the wall to score an out and perhaps steal a homerun by shagging the ball. Sometimes, after a catch is made and the ball protrudes half way out of the top, it's playfully called a snow cone.

Although Sammy is intrigued with the makeup of the catcher's mitt, he is most interested in the pitcher's glove that his Godfather gave him. The glove is not as small as the infield mitts. The weave is tight, he is told, for secrecy. One, to hold the appropriate grip around the ball without it being seen. The other function, to the disappointment of all those MLB lipreaders out there, is to cover the mouth during pitcher's mound discussions with his catcher and coaches.

Finally, studying the catcher's mitts, Sammy asks his Dad to explain the differences, and the catcher's knee/shin guards. The regular-sized catcher's mitt is meant to be able to catch a pain-free Fastball, dig it out of the dirt, when necessary, as well as get a quick throw to any bag that a runner attempts to steal; usually second base.

"But Dad, what is this really ginormous round one used for?"

"Sammy, there is a pitch called a Knuckle Ball. Although over the decades, technique and execution have in some ways improved or innovated the pitch somehow, the result is the same."

"Does the ball move, Dad?"

"Oh. . .It moves alright. Yeah. Especially under perfect weather conditions, like a slight breeze blowing into the pitcher's face, that Knuckle Ball floats, no spin, and because of that, the ball jumps erratically on the way to the plate. That is why the mitt here is so much larger than the others. No catcher wants to eat a face-full of Mississippi Mud. The ball really does move that much!

"It is a brave catcher who'll devote himself to a Knuckleballer, especially calling the game and typically act as Captain while he's at it. Let's not kid ourselves. There are several pitchers that built long careers, like Phil Niekro and Tim Wakefield throwing nothing but Knuckle Balls.

"Knuckleballers originally threw with their four fingernails locked behind the cross seam of the ball. I'd venture to say there aren't many of those throwers anymore, but believe me, Sammy," Dad finishes up for now. "Very few Knucklers are as effective as the originals, or just as effective enough, period. But, the Knuckle Ball is not going away, and if practiced, practiced, practiced, it can be a career pitch."

"Dad, I was looking at the shin guards."

"Yeah?"

"Look at this," Sammy holds up a guard. He points to a slightly bent and obviously sharpened buckle near the ankle.

"This looks kind of dangerous, Dad. Is it broken?"

"Oh Sammy, corruption exists almost everywhere. . .even in Baseball." Art fights to hold back on this subject.

"Those fuckin' Black Sox."

"So, what's it for?"

"The Spitball I explained to you was primitive in administration, uh, delivery. Everyone has tried the grease under the cap or brim, on the neck, under the tongue of the shoe, in the glove and under the belt. Some, even on the Rosin bag. All those, and many more failed for a simple reason; because they were easily detectable. The pitcher controls his own pitches. Do you know what I mean?"

"Yeah, Dad, and anyone caught throwing a Spitter is expelled immediately, and likely suspended?"

"You've got that right, Sammy."

"So, how does this blade equate to a Spitball?" The well-read boy asks.

"It was once considered ingenious. Instead of leaving the spit to the pitcher, every time the catcher pulls the ball out of his glove, he deceptively slices it across the blade, as you so aptly called it, when raising the ball to return to the pitcher. And every pitch thereafter is virtually unhittable."

"So, Dad, after only a few pitches, the batter's out! Ha!"

"Son, although the idea is ingenious, it is still illegal and against the rules. Besides that, nowadays catcher gear is vinyl, plastic and rubber. No metal."

"Yeah. But credit where due?"

"We better ask Pete Rose, heh?"

Art and his boy finish their Froot Loops and run out the kitchen door to the backyard for their daily practice.

"Hustle, hustle, hustle, Sammy! Atta boy! Run and squat; there you go! You're my man, Sam!

"My. . .

"Man. . .

"Sam!"

Dad gives Sammy three minutes, and then instructs calisthenics for encouragement. He leaves Sammy to run a few laps and sprint back and forth in the large yard. An acre of Costello's property in Portsmouth is surrounded by tall bamboo on two sides, and tall, thick, sweet honeysuckle on the other two. Both guys relax a short while. Sammy deserves a rest after his heavy workouts.

"Hey Dad, why don't we practice at the town softball field?" Sam asks.

"For one thing, it's hard to score a time slot. Plus, home offers flexibility." That much is true, but he adds that Sammy is in special training, and Dad does not wish to share that with others. He minces no words. Sammy is a sharp kid. Art's brand of training combines the shine his boy will one day elude and offers good fun along the way.

"Hey Dad, can we play Fungo? Please. . . before practice? Or maybe Pepper! Please?"

"Sure Sam. You want the glove or the bat? Or, we could both use a glove."

Mom comes outside and puts a tray of ice-cold lemonade on the picnic table. "You guys are already sweating outside, eh," she says in her leftover accent. "Oh, my, it is a hot one today."

Art and Sammy smile and thank Mom for the lemonade.

"Well, me and Dad are going to work out anyway," Sammy glances, smiling over at Art.

"We sure are, champ! Ready?"

Every day it is more and more clear that Art has a natural on his hands. He and son, Sammy, share something heady but also healthy, and his son seems to grow more muscular by the week. Meanwhile, Art can feel the goodness as he practices almost daily with Sammy.

"He's a damn good kid."

It's already come clear that Sammy will not be a catcher; he flinches. But, he shags balls out of the outfield with ease that appears angelic and often over the top of the outfield wall. However, Sammy absolutely excels in the infield. You can't get one by him at 2nd Base or Shortstop. Ever. Art takes to calling his son, "Scoop."

"I should note this for McDowell"

Sammy takes to the nickname just fine; it's just another identifier. His Dad chooses the 2nd Base position for Sam. He'll be in Little League in two years. He can field; he can hit; he can run; and he can slide.

And oh. . .what an arm!

Sammy continues to practice with Dad, who assures him it will all be worth it, and that he's still getting better and better with every practice.

5

Sammy often wonders why his time with his Godfather is so restricted but then, he reasons, Sam McDowell is traveling in The Show. Still, that doesn't thwart his asking the great player in front of Dad.

"Sammy," McDowell crouches down with Art. Looking Sammy straight in the eye, he says to both, "The sport is a roadshow all season long, approaching 170 games a year, or season. And in the off-season, where there is a little time to spend with family, there is Winter Ball and off-season practice. Sammy, it's an ever-enduring proposition."

Perhaps one of the most profound analogies for success that McDowell shares with Sammy is, "To achieve success, you better be damn sure you love what you're doing!"

"Sam," Art engages with the All-Star pitcher. "You have got to see our kid go! I practice almost daily with him. It's already become clear that Sammy will not be a catcher, because he flinches. *But*, he shags balls out of the outfield with such ease and finesse that he appears, in a way, ethereal. There's barely another way to describe him.

"However, Sam, our Sammy, completely excels in the infield. You can't get one by him. I've taken to calling him, 'Scoop.'"

Both men laugh and nod appreciatively.

His Dad puts Sammy at the 2nd Base position. "He'll be in Little League in two years. He can field; he can hit; he can run; and he can slide. And man! He has a strong arm!"

"Silly question, Art," McDowell begins. "Any talk of pitching at all?"

"Well Sam, he loves your high windup and delivery. The way you come way up and right over the top with that right-hand pitch. It tickles him every time."

"We have yet to test his pitching strength, but I suspect that time might well come soon. I mean. . .He's done all else and masterful at that! It will have been a natural progression of sorts when, or if, the conversation on pitching is raised."

It's been on Sammy's mind to reveal for two years, saving in thought only. It somehow feels like cheating. He has days of painful reluctance, full of question, and others full of promise and excitement. He'll report to Little League an All-Star hitting infielder, no doubt. As high man on the list, he's chosen by the most notorious basement team in the city leagues.

As much as his Dad tries to talk through it, Sammy is embarrassed and feels shortchanged. The team represents Kiwanis and is managed by two over-age, out-of-shape and literally demented brothers. They are merely a token team to represent the Kiwanis Club.

Few children, if any at all, put in the hours and daily practicing, rehearsing and carry around with them the high degree of integrity that Sammy does, so, he is being eaten inside out. He is smart enough to understand that the Top Pick goes to the previous season's bottom team. But he doesn't have to like it.

"Sammy, son, you have to play the game."

"I know, Dad. I know."

"If you become unhappy, we'll fix it.

"Look, Sammy," Dad continues. "You'll be in demand right from your first year, even more so the following season. You will lead an already established winning team. It's bound to happen. Believe me."

"OK, Dad," Says Sammy. "Sorry about being such a pudd over all this." Sammy stops but visible inertia from behind tells his Dad he's got more to say.

"Something else, Sammy?"

"Um," Sammy has a hard time bringing it up.

"Come on, Sammy. What is it, buddy?" Art coaxes.

"Dad, I've been practicing hard on my pitching skills."

"But, Sammy, seriously, you are groomed to take the ride through college, the Minors and into The Show based on all the work we've done and continue to do on the infield and batting practice."

"I've been studying and reading everything I can get my hands on. Dad. . .I really want to train as a pitcher. I've already begun. In the 90-minutes I wait for you to come home every day, for two years now, I'm throwing into the net."

"Really? Sammy? You have?"

"Yeah, Dad. I have a plan. You've got to hear this."

"Alright, Scoop." Art is a great Dad, easy to talk to, and work with.

"Of course, I'll ace all the must-haves, like the Fastball, Cutter, Curveball,

Knuckle-Curve, Slider, Multi-Seam Fastballs and other breaking balls."

"Yeah?"

"I am already close on all those already."

"No! Really?" Art says in disbelief. "Yeah, Sammy?"

"Yeah but *this* is the killer: Starting with a Cutter but implementing all innovations, I have almost mastered pronating the forearm!"

"The what?"

"I said pronating the forearm. Do you know what that is?"

Geez, it hits Art, what a cute kid, and so advanced.

"Yes, son. I do know what that is."

"I'll also have an unhittable arsenal. Gyroball, Screwball, Knuckle Ball, Foshball, the ancient Eephus Pitch and the Circle and Vulcan Change-ups."

"Wow, Sammy, you've been doing a lot of homework!"

"I want to concentrate on the pitches I can make-up that use pronating. Envision this: I'm a right-hander up against a right-side masher."

"Yeah? Go ahead."

"I've got him 1 and 2, and out of the pitcher's left side of a righty comes a Curveball the size of a Hawaiian wave, which at first confuses, then brushes the plate inside, or out, at the knees."

"So, he's called out or strikes out. I have to give it to you kid," Sammy's father says in a low, quiet voice. "You delivered a heck of a set up. Keep going."

"OK, Dad, I want to train as a pitcher but do

not want to debut in that role until Babe Ruth, college or Triple, Double or Single A ball."

"What brings this on? We've worked so hard on your fielding and hitting?"

"Besides throwing, I've been studying pitching for years, out of magazines, videos and books. I'm going to be a hero whether I throw three figures or junk and everything in between."

"Wow," Art leans back and lets himself rest on the lawn. "And what a surprise. Seriously, dude."

"So, can we go for it, Dad? If I keep up with my other roles in the meantime?"

"Sammy," his father says somberly. "Virtually all multi-positioner or multisport stars are forced out early because of injury."

"OK, Sammy," Dad calls out, all decked out in catcher's gear with the stop net behind him. "Follow my signals to start. 'One' is a Fastball; 'Two' is your basic Curveball -- nothing fancy just yet; and 'Three' is your Change-up, traditional. Follow my signals to throw to the designated locations; corners of the plate. Got it?"

"Yup! I got it, Dad!"

Art can't wait to see what his boy has worked out for himself so far. Today is all about target and speed. He squats. He calls for a simple Fastball down the middle. The ball comes right down the lane but the closer it gets to the plate it looks more like a chickpea. That's what velocity does to a baseball when thrown fast enough. The surprise makes Art blink, and upon impact, down he goes, right on his behind!

Sammy laughs out loud, but he tries to stifle it.

"Sorry, Dad."

"So, you've taught yourself some pitching."

"Yeah, Dad."

"Let's finish the drill. Give it all you've got."

"You going to be alright?"

"I think I can handle it, wise guy."

"Just took you by surprise, huh?"

"Exactly."

"Well, I told you."

Art calls for another Fastball to the right rear corner. Direct target hit with a smack and a thud. He calls for a Curveball and admits he's a tad frightened at what could happen next. He throws the signal down;

Sammy nods and delivers a classic Slider that perfectly cuts the plate diagonally in half. That pitch is usually thrown when you're looking for a strike out; down low.

Art can't help but grin at the Change-up, because Sammy went straight overhand, like a tribute to his Godfather delivering his own Fastball. Sammy throws a simple palm pitch that looks lobbed in and falling. But then, no: The pitch comes in slow, as a Change-up should in most cases, but at the last second it rises from the dirt past the batter's knees. Art has no idea how the heck Sammy did it, but he did. And then, does it again.

"Listen, Sammy," Art begins. "I want to get your Godfather up here to Portsmouth as soon as possible."

"Calling in the consultancy, Dad?"

"That's right, smart aleck."

Dad wants scientific. . .perhaps mathematic and objective-proven muscle analysis on progressive muscle growth at Sammy's age, as well as Sammy's other delivery options; first and foremost, and especially concerning the pronating forearm and wrist. McDowell fully agrees. Is there an obvious reason more pitchers do not implement it? Well, some do, but for fear of injury, seldom so.

"Geez, Art. I leave for a little while and this entire yard turns over. The kid's enthralled in it. Don't say I didn't tell you!"

Both men laugh, and over an ale at the picnic table, agree that they would support Sammy's dream, no matter how many times it could change. Look how well he did fielding and hitting.

"Sam, I got to tell you. Sammy's plan is a bit convoluted."

"How so, Art?"

"He has this idea that he'll continue in the infield through to maybe Double. . .Triple A ball."

"Oh, yeah?"

"Yeah, man. He has this grandiose strategy to carry on with 2nd base through mid-minors, and then, suddenly, bursts out this pitching phenom. . .like some weird fucking 'Jack-in-the-Box' being shot out of a cannon!"

"I agree that plan would hurt rather than help him. Not just as a player and athlete but his professional reputation; indecision cited."

"Good, Sam. So, we back each other on this aspect. Right?"

"Right Art. Right all the way."

6

Sammy chooses to change his mind about his role in Baseball over self-control, not some whimsical preference. His thoughts are stuck on how totally reactionary playing infield is. Sure, there are opportunities to make the occasional great play, but the entire sequence is laid out in front of an infielder for him, from the bat, to the diamond and finally to the out-base. Sammy wants more of a say in the direction and control of the game, particularly, between the Pitcher, the Batter, along with his Catcher.

He even signs the self-written document.

The secret sessions thrown every day the past two years that lead up to his infielder routines are paying off. He can see it. He can feel it, and he believes in himself.

"Should have seen Dad rock back on his behind off the first Fastball he signaled for!"

"Is that right, Art?" McDowell laughs.

"I cannot tell a lie, McDowell. Yup."

"So, our boy here has 'arm,' huh?"

"I sure do!" Sammy speaks right up.

"Sammy," McDowell has a question. "What have been some of your favorite reads on quirky pitchers. You're throwing Pronator a lot, so I know you've got to have other, let's say, spins up your jersey?"

At first glance, pitching a baseball looks simple. You raise your leg, rear back and let one fly. Of course, nothing could be further from the truth. Pitching is an art form, a complicated combination of specific, timed movements that involve multiple body parts working together in unison, concurrently, to create enough energy to send a projectile hurling 60-feet, 6-inches to home plate at a high speed. Everyone has a different way of reaching the same result, though some more bizarre and entertaining than others.

"I've read about Stu Miller because of the awesome Change-up he threw."

"You know, Sammy, his only ammo was that Change-up. Never threw over 67 miles per hour but his slow, slower and slowest Change-ups with a mean Change-up Curveball kept him in the majors for nearly two decades." McDowell adds.

"Not to mention all those saves he racked up." Sammy puts a cap on it; the bottom line.

"Have you looked at Ewell Blackwell at all? Heck of a Submariner."

"You know what I don't like about sidearm or underarm windups, like "The Whip" Blackwell's? It is that the windup movement alone gives the batter the sign right out of the hand. I don't think I'd ever opt to throw Submarines sidearm. . .even though it is one of the very few ways to get one to the plate. There are others I'd rather throw."

"There are pros and cons that come with sidearm pitching, but I like your thought process on this, Sammy. Smart kid!" He smiles at Art and ruffles Sammy's hair and they smile together.

"I read something interesting on Steve Hamilton," Sammy says. "He became a Mix-n-Mash fairly late in his career that lengthened it for him."

Hamilton was a 12-year veteran, primarily with the New York Yankees. Lefty Steve Hamilton saved 42 games in what was a solid but unspectacular career. Knowing that he needed to add something to his arsenal, Hamilton developed a pitch that he called the "Folly Floater." And the delivery of the pitch was a sight to behold. Drives batters crazy with it.

"Well worth his effort, I'd say, Sammy. . .You?"

"That's why I kept my notes on him.

"I read all about Paul Derringer. Man! Don't tell Dad I said this but that guy's delivery is definite Pitch Fuckery!"

"I recall Derringer," says McDowell. "He was a six-time All-Star who won 223 games over a 15-year career, primarily with the Cincinnati Reds. And you are right on the money: Paul

Derringer used *deception* to befuddle batters from 1931 through 1945.

"The deceptive part of Derringer's game was in his delivery. When he had his right arm behind him as he prepared to throw, his left leg blocked the batter's view of his right hand. So, it wasn't until the ball was fully released that the batter had a chance to key in on it."

"I read about Ted Abernathy because I saw his comeback referenced somewhere. His story reminded me to never give up."

"Right Sammy. Ted was a relief pitcher who played for seven teams over a 14-year career, picking up 148 saves along the way. Originally, he threw from a three-quarters arm angle, but a serious shoulder injury forced him to re-invent himself—which he did, as a hybrid Sidearm/Submarine pitcher. But watch him, Sammy, really, it was more of a hybrid *underhand* pitching motion than anything else, and it drove hitters nuts as his Curveball rose and his Fastball sank."

"Cincinnati Reds ace Johnny Cueto finds success by utilizing a delivery that is seldom used in the game today." Sammy reads.

"Cueto twists his entire body around so that he's facing second base, then twists back around and the ball *explodes* toward the plate!"

"Unlike others who have utilized this motion in the past," McDowell says. "Cueto looks toward and spooks the batter just before releasing the pitch."

McDowell says to Sammy, "Luis Tiant could throw a Fastball, Curveball, Slider, Knuckle Ball, Palm Ball and a Slow Curve, bringing his arm either over the top, three-quarters or sidearm."

"Well yeah," Sammy adds. "And on top of that, Tiant would almost turn around to face second base during his windup but instead of spinning back around and firing the ball toward home plate in a fluid motion, he'd hesitate, often looking around the park before throwing his pitch."

"It made it nearly impossible for batters to figure out what was coming, as they not only couldn't tell what pitch he was throwing but they had no clue as to what arm angle he was going to use to throw it, never mind the timing and target." McDowell offers.

"Awesome!" Sammy says. "Wow!"

"Scariest pitcher I ever faced," McDowell declares. "I swear. Scary. I shit you not."

The conversation turns to the great Juan Marichal. A 10-time All-Star and member of the Hall of Fame, Juan Marichal spent 14 of his 16 years in the majors with the San Francisco Giants, throwing a no-hitter in 1963 and intimidating batters every time he toes the rubber.

"His 191 victories during the 1960s led all pitchers, and part of his success can be attributed to the fact that Marichal was a master of intimidation, often throwing at batters' helmets to remind them that he owned the plate and would throw wherever he liked, whenever he liked."

"Oh. . .The Bean Ball. . .Just like my Bean Ball" Sammy replies.

"Marichal's leg kick is the unique part of his windup and delivery," McDowell continues. "He not only gets his leg incredibly high, but the leg is almost *vertical* when he starts to move forward. As with others on this list, Marichal's delivery hid the ball from the view of batters, giving them absolutely no time to pick up the ball.

"Next, Sammy?" McDowell asks.

"Hideo Nomo, for his windup and delivery." Sammy reads.

"The National League Rookie of the Year and the only Japanese pitcher to throw a no-hitter in the major leagues; a feat he accomplished twice. Hideo Nomo had a bizarre delivery."

"I remember watching Hideo," says McDowell. "Nomo would raise both arms straight above his head, twist his body toward second base, then spin around toward home and release the pitch. Watching was like watching freaking Japanese fireworks!

"Why Dean Chance, Sammy?"

"For his hidden delivery," Sammy replies. "As soon as he would get the sign from the catcher and start his windup, he would twist around so that his back was facing home plate—and the batter.

"Chance would then spin around and fire the ball toward the plate, often never getting more than a faint glimpse beforehand of where the catcher was set up. Hitters not only had no idea what pitch was coming, they had no idea where the pitch was headed, since whether Chance actually looked at home plate before throwing the ball was that unclear."

"Good Lord!"

"Let me guess this one, Sammy," McDowell says. "Jim Abbott: If he can do it, so can I."

"Pretty much." Sammy affirms.

One of the great feel-good stories in sports history, Jim Abbott, who was born without a right hand, not only pitched in the major leagues but he threw a no-hitter as well.

Never thinking of himself as disabled or handicapped, Abbott figured out how to play his position. During his delivery, he would balance his glove on his right arm, with the ball in his left hand. As soon as the hand released the ball, he'd quickly put the glove on his left hand, so he was prepared to field.

"Incredible, huh Sammy?"

"For sure! I also looked way back at Carl Hubbell; 'Mr. No Fear.' He was an eight-time All-Star, two-time National League MVP and a member of the Hall of Fame, plus, almost unheard of today, Carl Hubbell spent his entire 16-year career with one team; the New York Giants."

"Listen to this!" Sammy reads out loud from his notebook.

"In the 1934 All-Star Game, Hubbell struck out five Hall of Famers in a row: Babe Ruth,

Lou Gehrig, Nellie Fox, Al Simmons and Joe Cronin, relying on his favorite pitch, the Screwball."

Hubbell's delivery was so violent that by the time he retired in 1943 at the age of 40, his left arm had been permanently disfigured and pulled apart from the abuse he put it through.

"What in the world is Mark Fidrych doing in here, pal?" McDowell asks incredulously.

"He's my reminder to not take myself too seriously and to keep fun in the game."

"Mark 'The Byrd' Fidrych may not belong on this list," McDowell says. "Merely considering his antics on display in between pitches but you can't compile a list involving quirky pitchers and *not* mention Mark Fidrych. So, I get it, I do get it now."

"Right," Sammy continues. "His career

lasted only five years due to injury, but he will forever be remembered as one of the most entertaining and loved players the game has ever seen. He belongs up there with the goofy, legendary Jimmy Piersall.

"On the mound, Fidrych would talk to himself. He'd talk to the ball. Sometimes, he'd stand on the mound and hold the ball as if he were about to throw a dart at a Homeplate-dartboard. Other times, he'd crouch down on the mound and begin to smooth out the cleat marks left by others. Announcers coined the act a Mound Manicure. If a ball had been hit too many times, he'd refuse to pitch until it was removed from the game."

"Like I said, you can't possibly write about quirky Baseball players and not include Mr. Mark Fidrych (R.I.P.). And what an all-around good guy he is, uh. . . he was."

THE SAMMY SQUAD

7

After a conference call with McDowell and
New York friend Tom Seaver, Art takes away an
idea that will either make his boy fly like an
eagle or sink like a bottom fish. They come
to a consensus that given Sammy's readiness,
he should come out pitching next season. If
he's not yet got it, play him at 2nd Base.

"Hey Sammy," Art calls. "We've got a little
less than one more year before Little League
starts next season. I had a conference call
with your Godfather and another star you may
remember, New York Met friend Tom Seaver."

"Tom Seaver?"

"Yep."

"Wow, this is awesome!"

"I want to take an inventory of everything you've got. That means what you've got rock solid. You can throw it right. . .perfect. . . every time and hit your target. I also want to talk about what you ultimately want, and what you studied behind windup and delivery. I know you went through the routines with your Godfather. Have you decided on a delivery?"

"Yes, Dad," Sammy answers. "We came up with a hybrid windup that equally hides the ball and spooks the batter. Loosely, somewhat like Paul Derringer's and Luis Tiant's deliveries."

"Excellent, Sammy, I'm going to want to see it some more. This is a huge change of plan, son. Leave it at that, so no jinxing."

"Don't you want to see my menu, Dad?"

"Yes, of course I do, or should I dare?" Art jokes.

"OK Sammy, get set on your mound. I'll see what I can do about memorizing your signals while I gear up." Art laughs out loud.

They start off by playing catch, then throwing from the stretch down to the crouch. Fastballs, Curveballs and Change-ups only to start with.

"I don't want to get knocked onto my backside again!" Art laughs. "Now, let's see your windup. Throw Fastballs, Curves and Change-ups."

Sammy winds-up consistently no matter the oncoming pitch. He and his Dad continue the windups and stick with the pitch trio they use to warm-up.

Sammy keeps the ball deep in the mitt as he musters his fingers into the grip. He moves both arms together until nearly the very release itself. It appears he will never get the pitch out of the pocket, like it's glued into the basket, but he has practiced this movement hundreds of times.

The first and only glimpse of the ball is the nanosecond between the outer windup or stretch and when the ball is already half way to the plate.

"My goodness, son," Art stands up and says. "That is one scary release. I'm not kidding!"

"And I do it all without having to turn to 2nd Base. I just have to ready my throwing arm for that flash."

"It actually struck me with an instant of imbalance. . .fear even."

"I could loosen up on the windup and gain just a little more ball speed, but I think the element of surprise outweighs the velocity."

"Considering your menu, I think that is a wise choice, Sammy."

Art calls his son over to the picnic table. The time has come to review Sammy's menu. His Dad is aware of some of the flings but hardly familiar with others. Sammy and his Dad each have a set list in front of them. Like they're ready to order lunch at a New Jersey diner.

"OK Sammy," Art says. "Let's go down the list one-by-one. I want you to concentrate and tell me how you feel about each pitch. What is your comfort level? Are they under control: Can you hit the target? And finally, how your body feels. . .your arm. And I want the truth. You got it?"

Sammy and his Godfather had whittled down a complete list to what they feel are the best twelve or so to start with.

"OK Dad. Here's what Godfather, Tom and I came up with. Here we go.

"Slider, because it is underrated, therefore unexpected. When I give it that good movement and good location, it's remarkably untouchable. It can also stand as the third fastest pitch in Baseball after only the two top Fastballs. Ted Williams called the Slider "the greatest pitch ever." I have this pitch under control traditionally and pronator.

"Knuckle-Curve, because no one believes you when you say you throw one but it's like a Curveball on steroids. The index finger just creates more spin than a regular Curveball, providing an even more dominant Curveball, thus more strikeouts. The Knuckle-Curve messes up a batter mentally. No one likes a

Knuckle-Curve, except the pitcher. I struck Godfather out every time with it. However, I just must get a good enough spin on it. I have this pitch under control traditionally and pronator.

"Four-Seam Fastball, because everyone knows that players base their entire arsenal of Fastballs on this specific pitch. The heck is this: when someone pitches one of these, it's a dinger, because the ball doesn't move. It takes impeccable location and speed to throw a successful Four-Seamer. I do not plan on depending on it, but I won't blow-off a call from the bench either."

"Of course not." Tom says.

"Two-Seam Fastball, because it is the 2nd fastest pitch, *and* it moves on the hitter. I have this pitch under control traditionally and pronator.

"Curveball, because every pitcher in the world, college level and up must have one. And they must have at least one. I have several versions of this pitch, based on arc and speed, under control traditionally and pronator. You should see a batter dance when they see one coming!

"Split-Finger-Fastball or Splitter, because it's so easy to throw, it's a great pitch and does not put pressure on your arm like a Curveball or Slider will from time to time. It's just a hazard of the business. Splitters are great pitches. They break enough to get any batter out with the proper timing and location.

"Gyroball, because while it's not a magic pitch by the elders, it behaves like one. It gets in a batter's head. When executed properly, from the batter's POV, it's rising, when it's actually dropping. Wait till you see it. It's astonishing! I have this pitch under control traditionally and pronator.

"Screwball, because pronator or traditionally thrown, there's crazy movement that will beat out a three and two every time it's thrown low across the plate.

"Change-up, because it is the true cornerstone of a pitcher's repertoire; never a bad time for a Change-up. I have several versions of this pitch under control traditionally and pronator. Dad, Godfather Sam says the pronator spin makes batters think they're seeing things."

"I bet it does!"

"Okay. Knuckle Ball, because given the weather and if kept down low, it's strike-out time. It's a tricky pitch, and prone to be hit for homers if left up high in the zone. Otherwise, it's very hard to hit and is a well-rounded pitch. It's been my toughest pitch to learn. But it is just like throwing a whiffle ball. It will break at least three or four times before reaching the plate. The inner cork kernel has a mind of its own.

"I decided against a Sinker or Submarine, or anything thrown sidearm because they're too easy to see coming.

"Cutter: What can I say, Dad? Why isn't this the number one for every pitcher out there? Once one pitcher revolutionized it, other pitchers, year by year find out the wonders of this pitch. You think it is a Fastball, then, *surprise*, it breaks away, or in. I have this pitch under control traditionally and pronator.

"I'm throwing it at my age, and it doesn't hurt my arm in any way, and it strikes batters out 9 out of 10 times. It really tricks the hitter because it looks like a

Fastball coming straight in but then, *doink*, it moves. I love this pitch!

"The Spitball uses moisture to alter the shape of the ball, making it into an oblong and virtually impossible to hit. This pitch is so nasty it is banned from the league. And pitchers and catchers still figure out ways to pull it off. I don't plan on using it. . .yet. My only idea is to keep it simple, openly, solely and commonly use the sweat off my brow, head, ears and neck. Nothing illegal with that.

"Eephus Pitch, because this pitch really does drop on the batter like no other, and looks like a clown pitch, best used on heavy hitters. It reaches the plate and drops like a peppermill out of a cocky chef's hand.

"Foshball, because this great pitch is very much like a Splitter but with some tail away from a right-handed batter or left if thrown pronator. There are technically two ways to grip it as well, both resulting in the same movement but with different speed. Downright good pitch but very underrated, and rarely seen. I have traditional control and pronator.

"Circle Change-up, because this is an amazing cross between a Change-up and a Sinker. It's the *only* Sinker I'll throw, besides the Eephus."

"You've compiled quite a repertoire Sammy!"

"Thanks, Dad. I know there are more than ten but some of these pitches are too great against a batter and so easy to pitch, I can't pass them up or count them out.

"Oh yeah, Dad, forgot to mention my Bean Ball."

8

Dad has another take on unleashing Sammy's pitching prowess. He first wants to play him at 2nd base with a pitcher option, which is legal in Divisional Little League and City Leagues, such as Babe Ruth. He's reviewing the regular season rules.

Regular Season Pitching Rules

Baseball

VI PITCHERS

(a) Any player on a regular season team may pitch. (NOTE: There is no limit to the number of pitchers a team may use in a game.)

(b) A pitcher once removed from the mound cannot return as a pitcher. Junior, Senior, and Big League

Divisions only: A pitcher remaining in the game but moving to a different position, can return as a pitcher anytime in the remainder of the game but only once per game.

(c) The manager must remove the pitcher when said pitcher reaches the limit for his/her age group as noted below but the pitcher may remain in the game at another position:

League Age 17-18 105 pitches per day

13-16 95 pitches per day

11-12 85 pitches per day

9-10 75 pitches per day

7-8 50 pitches per day

Exception: If a pitcher reaches the limit imposed in Regulation VI (c) for his/her league age while facing a batter, the pitcher may continue to pitch until any one of the following conditions occurs:

1. That batter reaches base;

2. That batter is put out;

3. The third out is made to complete the half-inning. Note 1: A pitcher who delivers 41 or more pitches in a game cannot play the position of catcher for the remainder of that day.

(d) Pitchers league age 14 and under must adhere to the following rest requirements:

• If a player pitches 66 or more pitches in a day, four (4) calendar days of rest must be observed.

• If a player pitches 51-65 pitches in a day, three (3) calendar days of rest must be observed.

- If a player pitches 36-50 pitches in a day, two (2) calendar days of rest must be observed.

- If a player pitches 21-35 pitches in a day, one (1) calendar days of rest must be observed.

- If a player pitches 1-20 pitches in a day, no (0) calendar day of rest is required.

"Hmmm," Art takes a breath. "Pitchers league age 15-18 must adhere to the following rest requirements. Blah, blah, blah. . .We're looking good, Sammy."

9

Sammy's original idea of playing 2nd throughout his Little League seasons is not far off from where his father is with the decision to pitch. Referring to the Season Rule Guideline, he thinks of an idea. The rule he is trying to work into Sammy's and the manager's advantage. Of course, they can pitch Sammy exclusively, too.

"Hey Sammy?"

"Yeah Dad?"

"I want you to know that I read your short credo on the merits of the pitcher's role against those of the infield."

"Um, you did?" Sammy gulps.

"I just want you to know that I respect that, man. Everyone is behind you one-hundred percent."

"That's great, Dad. Thanks!"

"You got it, Scoop."

A manager may swap pitchers off and back on the mound if the player remains in the game at some position or the other. This is huge. He calls the new team manager and gets Sammy to join them. He opens a couple of beers for him and the manager, and then shares with him what Sammy has been working on for the past two years. Art offers a demonstration.

First, they perform an array of infield routine workouts. The team manager is beyond impressed at Sammy's talent at 2nd Base, as well as his hitting.

"Now, there's this," Art says. "Everything you witness here today is hush-hush. Nobody can know. Do we have an agreement?"

"OK, that's a deal, Art."

"Have you seen enough infield play for now? Does he look like a starter to you?"

"You bet he does!" He replies, and says to Sammy, "You've been working awfully hard on your Baseball, haven't you?"

"Yes, sir," Sammy answers quietly. "I sure have."

"Well, we've got a surprise for you, skipper." Art says.

"Is that so?"

"Darn sure do!" Art speaks right up.

"Go prep your mound, Sammy. I'll gear up to catch for you."

"What in the. . ." The manager is taken

aback but keen as can be on what he thinks he's about to see.

"Mr. Marusso, please take this set list. Sammy will begin at the top and work his way to the bottom. He'll throw three of each pitch listed. Those pronator, he'll throw six. We'll take short breaks between each pitch set. Got it? Ready?"

"Pronator? What? Pronator?"

"OK Sammy: Fastball"

The smack and thud the ball makes upon impact lets everyone know the pitch has speed.

"Wait. Wait!" Marusso yells, running across the yard toward the driveway. "I have to go get my radar gun! I'll be right back. One minute."

"Oh gwad. Do-over Sammy."

"He's throwing 77 miles an hour!"

"Hold on here. Sammy break. Mr. Marusso, please follow me."

Art walks Marusso to the garage and up to a steel 'tall boy' wardrobe dresser. He pulls out a Major League umpire-rated chest pad, a pair of knee/shin guards, and a face mask. He hands them all to Marusso. As the manager suits up, Art explains again that this is a private demonstration. It's not about analysis of any or every pitch thrown.

"But I want you to have the opportunity to witness a demo, because Sammy is likely coming your way. So, take your stance behind me. I'll announce the pitch and you observe. Keep your eye on the ball." Art chuckles. "We'll save any discussion until the demo is complete. Are you with me on this, Manager?"

"Yes. I apologize. Let's give it another

go. I want to see a moving ball!" Marusso lets out a belly laugh.

"By the way," Art asks. "What was the speed of that last Fastball?"

"78 miles an hour."

"Here comes a Knuckle-Curve."

The manager Marusso is absolutely stunned.

Art is reviewing the team rosters to see who's coming back, who's graduating to Babe Ruth, and anyone who is coming in or going away for whatever reason. There are only two pitchers in the division who have anything going for them. Eug Aman throws a *fast* Fastball for his age that no one can hit unless it's by luck. Just stick the bat out there and see what happens. His Breaking Ball is fair at best.

Dean Lundquist is a big, beefy lefty with a round-house Curveball that scares the crap out of everybody facing him. His Fastball is not quite comparable to Aman's. Aman's Fastball is the undisputed best in the division to date. All batters have is that Aman has control. He won't bean them. Every kid out there is afraid to face Lundquist because of his size, he is a lefty and that huge Curve.

The question is, how to insert Sammy into the League. Art wants to give him the introduction he deserves. The 'utility pitcher' idea makes sense, perhaps, but puts more of an onus on the integrity of the rest of the rag-tag, bottom floor team.

Art has Sammy invite Jimmy Presta over to begin pitcher/catcher team conditioning. Art thinks that as soon as Presta sees what Sammy has, he'll know they have a winning combination. And everybody likes a winner. Art, McDowell and Seaver are all in for Sammy debuting as the pitcher he is. If Presta can handle the load, it's a done deal. Besides Sammy and Art, Jimmy is thrilled to meet and talk to Sam McDowell and Tom Seaver. He understands what the stakes are here, and he feels proud and happy to be part of it.

"who the heck ever heard of pronator muscle pitching, anyway?"

One thing the premier pitchers have against the pitch numbers rules is that it takes very few pitches to drop each batter. While Sammy and Jimmy practice, Art keeps an eye out for the essential rudiments they cannot let slip. They compose various sets of pitches to serve each opposing batter. Naturally, this exercise gets finer tuned as the season moves forward. For the returning players, Sammy and Jimmy have all the ammo they need.

10

Under watchful eyes, Sammy and Jimmy faithfully perform their routine workouts five days a week. Art lets them choose their own solo workouts, but they must be ready to work through the menu formally by the time Art arrives home. They are expected to be on schedule and ready to continue the current stress-points on every subsequent afternoon.

It stands to expectation that Sammy, but more so Jimmy, take to the most difficult pitches, or any pitch or catch that may not be up to par. Sammy knows more than anyone how a well-thrown pitch should behave and certainly how any one pitch makes his arm feel. Jimmy works extra hard to keep up and understand Sammy, and his continuing his sequential approach during each leg of their workouts.

Jimmy is a year older than Sammy. He started Little League last year. He is a leading hitter and the starting catcher: That's where he began and that's where he will stay. Kiwanis, however, must develop another catcher if Jimmy is to be made available to catch any time and every time Sammy takes the mound, or is in the bull pen.

Kiwanis is assigned the Mary Dondero School yard for their practice time. There is no diamond groomed out there, but the team does their best to hack one out. Art borrowed a couple of machines from Public Works. Art donates the plate and bags and makes sure the team has lye and a push liner to mark the foul lines and other bounds.

"Coach Marusso," Art calls out from the entrance gate and waves at the team manager, who is standing at 3rd Base. "Do you have a few minutes to chat?"

"Sure. Art. What's up?" With Art, it's usually something at the least. . .interesting.

"I have news of a development, designed by McDowell, Seaver and me."

"I'm all ears, Art."

"We believe Sammy should be a starting pitcher from the get-go. The idea to bring him on and off by bouncing him on and off 2nd Base has raised some concern. Relief pitcher and a Closer are obviously acceptable."

"So, I thought it might." Marusso says.

"Good! We want Sammy to play pitcher

exclusively. We all know that the more you shuttle players around the field, and the more roles he's called on to play, the more margin for injury widens. Not to mention errors. That alone is enough to bring the issue to the table."

"I would also tend to agree without question."

"Also, and this is ultimately for Sammy's benefit, we believe he deserves a proper introduction to the Division as the extraordinary pitcher that he is. He developed his own windup, stretch, menu of pitches, and most of all his pronator mechanics. We do not plan to dictate anything out of the usual or about his talent. We can let all that speak for itself."

"That's on-field class, Art," Marusso replies. "Classy indeed."

"OK. That's it for now, and so as not to jinx, no speaking about specific plans for Sammy and Jimmy beyond their presence on the roster. That's it."

"I fully concur with every bit of what you guys came up with," Marusso says. "And you can count on me, my full support, in the future, too. Let's consider it done."

The day is here. It represents the last formal tutelage with Art, Sammy and Jimmy from Seaver and McDowell. Everyone sits around the picnic table. The subject today has been touched on but not emphasized enough considering its importance; pitch sequence. A pitcher can't just throw their best sequence repeatedly, and at the very least, if they do repeat a pitch, location must be different. The hitter has his eyes on the ball but keeping him guessing on location makes all the difference in the world. His eyes play tricks on him.

Art introduces McDowell and Seaver as the stars of the show. They've agreed to appear via teleconference, as they trade-off opinions, know-how, good pitching sense and largely the importance of pitching sequence and location.

Art opens with: "Pitch Sequence: What to throw and when? So, what's the best pitch sequence? What pitches should be thrown and when should you throw them?

"Tom, why don't you start things up."

"I wish pitching was that easy; throwing my three best pitches. You get a guy 0-1 with an outside Fastball and then automatically throw a Curveball for strike two. Unfortunately, that's not the way it is.

"To be successful pitchers, we must mix up our pitch sequence. There is no certain formula for what pitches to throw and when to throw them. If there were, then everybody'd be a winner! Every batter and every situation are different. You want to add to that McDowell?"

"Yes, I do. Tom is right. There are a few things that you must know about pitch sequence and mixing up your pitches.

"Number one: As you get into higher levels of Baseball, the scouting reports become more specific. You can expect every hitter on the other team to know exactly what percent of Fastballs, Curveballs, and Change-ups that you throw in each count. Therefore, the more you mix it up, the more you'll keep them guessing.

"Number two: Changing eye levels, throwing up and down, and disrupting the hitter's balance, throwing in and out, and disrupting the hitter's timing, throwing fast and slow, are *the* best ways to mix up your pitches. For example, throwing an up and in Fastball will make the down and away Curveball thrown a very tough pitch to hit."

"OK, let me add something to that," Tom says.

"Number three: Doubling up on pitches is not necessarily a bad thing. Sometimes it's good to go back to back on an inside Fastball, or maybe even two Curveballs low and away. It will keep hitters guessing even more if you can effectively throw these pitches for strikes. Just remember, if you are throwing an off-speed pitch back to back, the second one *must* be 'lower and slower' than the first.

"McDowell?"

"Number four: Never throw your worst

off-speed pitch after your best off-speed pitch. Let's take for example a pitcher who throws a Fastball, Curveball, and a Change-up. Let's say that this pitcher's best pitch is his Fastball, followed by his Curveball, and then his Change-up is his least effective pitch. This pitcher should never throw a Change-up after a Curveball. The reason for this is because the pitcher will speed up the hitter's bat with his Curveball and have him ready to hit his 3rd best pitch which is around the same speed. The batter will be licking his lips as that Change-up comes floating in.

"Tom? Closing comment?"

"Yes. Thank you. Those are just a few things to think about when it comes to pitch sequence and mixing up your pitches. Like it was said before, there is no secret formula on what pitch to throw and when to throw it, however, these few tips should help you out with developing your own pitch sequences and pitching philosophy.

"Your *voice!*"

11

Art hires his friends at Diversified Pools to build an alley in the yard so that Sammy and Jimmy can practice all winter long. Art has seen the wonders the guys at Diversified do with heavy plastic tarps and studs as they build in-ground pools twelve months a year.

Working off specs drawn up by Art, the job turns out perfectly. He buys a couple space heaters that blow enough heat to keep it comfortably warm in the pen.

"Throw me that Fastball quick and dirty!" Jimmy yells at Sammy.

"How about immediate and filthy!" And before Sammy can finish, the ball is in Jimmy's glove.

This season, Art assigns the pitcher/catcher pair one major task, based on the last meeting with McDowell and Seaver: *Location!*

"OK Jimmy," Sammy says. "Mix the pitches up. Just give me the sign. But, move the location within pitch sequences as unpredictable as well as predictable. Let's imagine we've got a batter. And you are the mind and eyes of that batter, OK?"

"This is going to be fun, Sammy!"

Jimmy accepts and fully admits he still has trouble with the pronator throws. Some, like the Cutter, appear more a natural movement of the ball but others, most in fact, still fool the otherwise adept catcher.

So, the two boys must build those workouts comingled with the assignments from Art,

McDowell and Seaver. Sammy let's his Dad know what he and Jimmy talk about. Dad understands completely and gives Sammy his blessing. A pressing approval but an approval nonetheless.

Sammy gets the sign for a pronator round-house Curve. He takes his time, performs his windup, and pulls the backward spin down. The ball leaves his grip looking like a broken Fastball that a kid doesn't know how to throw. It immediately arcs way out to the pitcher's left. It seems to hang there but Jimmy can see it coming in at about seventy miles an hour. The ball breaks to the right and down. Jimmy catches it but admits it was a discomforting play.

"Geez Sammy," Jimmy yells. "You are a freaking twisted spinster!"

"Ha, ha, ha, ha, ha! Is *that* my new nick name?"

"No man. Just saying," Jimmy answers. "Your pronators are nothing short of mind-blowing."

"Good, because I don't like that name." Sammy says. "It sounds like an antique metal band. *You* are effing funny Jimmy Presta. Good catch."

"Still shaky inside but I'm feeling better with every practice."

"Listen, Jimmy. Just keep calling the problem pitches, pronator or not. Now, let's go."

Art and Coach Marusso feel like they're walking on egg shells. Even the team mates do not know, and some may never know what Sammy and Jimmy bring to the team. Even though Kiwanis is under new management, the rest of the division continue to blow them off and make fun. Oh, kids can be cruel but the opposing Coaching staffs play along, as well. Pitiful bums.

"Frustrated, fallen heroes all."

Every team has a full starting roster carried over from last season. No one has even one pitcher that can make a difference. This is Aman's and Lundquist's last qualifying year but obviously, they are both bigger and stronger than last season. No pitchers besides them pose any threat. Art and Marusso have their attention on the hitting talent and batting stats.

They go about their process in friendly, stealth ways, such as bringing popsicles and Gatorade to opposing team practices. They set a tone of simple chit-chat around their fact gathering: The mentality is like honor among thieves. The other Coaches openly condescend over Marusso. Art warns of this, and the two are ready to take it and laugh along.

They bring along faux rosters to bait the other Coaches that are making fun of them, to share their pre-season team rosters and stats. The best Art can do is rely on his and Marusso's memory to enter the other teams' data into the Tablet they have in the truck. The app they use takes the raw data input and turns it into meaningful output information.

Art decides to keep Sammy and Jimmy secluded in his yard the first half-a-dozen team practices. He wants them walking onto the field, or into the bull pen fully relaxed, in the know and completely fearless. All the kids on the team will, during practice, eventually face Sammy, and even if the ball movement does not spook them, they will know there is something funky going on.

No announcements are to be made to highlight the talent, know-how or impact of Sammy's menu and style. Most team mates are immediately fearful of his windup. Marusso as often as possible tends to utilize his other pitchers for batting practice. Sammy is put in more to observe what he is doing, not the batters. And that can be done from within the bull pen.

Marusso is a one-man show but a very good one, if not a dite outdated. Art is busy recruiting a team of Coaches to handle special operations, such as hitting, throwing, fielding and running. He decides and tells Marusso that he'd like to take the pitching Coach role.

Between Art and Marusso, they come up with and can bring on two additional utility Coaches. Physically, they may be kept the busiest of all but are no more or less important than the rest of the Coaching staff. . .and players.

Kiwanis has five new-comers who are excellent in the field and are natural born hitters. During one of the first practices, Marusso makes it clear and understood by all that they will play as a team and win as a team, regardless of who hits, who steals, who pitches or who makes the 'great play.' The Coach's applause reigns in a circle of cheering players.

Art is noticeably critical of the 2nd base fielder but decides he likes what he sees. There are no infielders as sharp as Sammy but with some hard work they can be developed. They've got a six-foot-three first-baseman who bats clean-up. The Shortstop, 2nd baseman and 3rd baseman open the lineup: They excel at base hits and base-running. The outfielders make up the last of the lineup, and two out of three are genuinely big, bad power hitters.

Art must admit that he does indeed see a winning team.

12

It's opening day at Leary Field and Kiwanis faces Moose, the top performing team of the prior season. It is scheduled the first game of the day, and it's no coincidence that the Division officials cast the worst team of last season up against the best. Moose is the Home team so take the field first.

Their starting pitcher is an average height, overweight boy who throws nothing but Fastballs, Curves and Change-ups. It's obvious that they do not feel they need anyone stronger against Kiwanis. But Kiwanis is not insulted. They came to play. They now know *how* to play.

The first three batters hit for singles, scoring one, and their clean-up hitter is at the plate. Moose's manager visits the mound, chats for a moment, slaps the pitcher on the back side and trots back to the dugout. He plans on catching up on bat characteristics. No problem.

The Kiwanis 1st baseman, Jay Barfield, stands there as calm as can be and watches a Fastball zip by. He then sees a curve coming in and rests his bat on his right shoulder. He expects the Change-up that comes in next.

It is as slow a pitch as he's ever seen, and there is no movement. The ball comes right down the lane, on the high side, and Barfield swings. By the time the fielders look above at the ball flying over their heads, it lands on the lawn over the center field fence and slowly rolls under a car parked there.

Two out of the next two Kiwanis batters ground out, and batter seven strikes out. Kiwanis runs out to the field full of confidence. They are winning 4-0 after half an inning. They are not even a shadow of the team they were last year.

As the fielders warm up, Sammy and Jimmy leisurely pass the ball back and forth, as the umpire watches curiously. They're dancing holding a chicken by the neck. And there's enough adrenaline and testosterone on the grounds out there that the Kiwanis round the horn warm-ups appear quick, fast and sharp, almost like MLB.

Moose comes up to bat. Sammy throws his Bean Ball. It is a high, inside 78 MPH Fastball that rocks the batter back and off-balance.

The umpire points at Sammy and tells Jimmy to "watch it."

In comes a knee-high Fastball called for a strike. Another Fastball sails toward the plate and the batter cocks his bat ready to swing. The Fastball breaks inward at the knees and the batter whiffs. A Change-up comes in moving but because it looks slow, the batter swings late, pops-up and fouls out on the first base line.

Kiwanis comes back up near the top of the lineup. Moose leaves their pitcher in place. This time, he gets an infield runner thanks to a double by Barfield, and then an infield out, and a fly out.

Moose comes up with the middle of the order. Sammy and Jimmy put their sequence into play. In comes a Slider for a called strike. The batter then fans on a Change-up. Jimmy calls for a Knuckle Ball. The batter just stands there, eyes darting side to side and up and down, totally disoriented. He doesn't know where to level his swing, so he takes a called strike.

The game rhythm stays that way all seven Little League innings. Kiwanis scores another in the 7th inning. Moose hitters are shut-out. In the middle of the final inning, with Kiwanis leading 5-0, the Moose manager calls time, comes out of the dugout and walks over to the home plate umpire, who meets him half way.

"Listen ump, there is something, uh, funny going on here," the Moose manager says. "I want the game balls inspected."

"Well now, Moose, I'll tell you what's going on," the ump says impatiently. Ugh! He does not like whiners. "Kiwanis has game. Period. Get used to it. Truth; straight out of Mr. Umpire!"

"Well, what about that Beaner thrown in the first?"

The ump, pulls-off his mask and almost flung his hat to the ground (Prop magic: If thrown, that one would dismiss the coach) tries to explain patiently.

"The Bean ball is used strategically to lay a fear that the Pitcher is just a bad one throwing at them. Come-on man! Get your game gathered and stop trying to blame a winning team for leading victorious."

Opposing coaches try everything they can to somehow disqualify Art, Sammy and Jimmy. It becomes wisdom in mind, a weekly ritual but with Art right there, rule books in hand, there is no chance on Earth *that* is ever going to happen. Sammy has the sequences down pat and wants to throw some pronator. He starts and wins four games but wants to give pronator a chance to shine.

Kiwanis, with Art debating every challenge, is proven clean, fair and square. They face Lions this afternoon. Most the players are carry-overs from last year, so Sammy and Jimmy are quite prepared to sweep. It is the perfect game to throw pronators. Sammy throws a lot of Sliders, Cutters, Change-ups and Curves.

Applying the pronator arm movement is ruinous and destructive to the Lions' batting lineup. Jimmy is mixing signs and locations, exactly as told and planned. The first two pitches or two come in close, just brushing the plate. The balls come in at about 55 MPH, slow for Sammy, and he catches them missing, taking or fouling out.

Those who can see the difference in the third pitch will go on to tell numerous people, numerous times, that Sammy has some kind of voodoo-ball going on. Sammy allows two runs from singles hit to the outfield. Lions are hitting his Fastball. The score is tied at two all when in the top of the 7th, Barfield homers to put Kiwanis on top.

In the bottom of the seventh, Sammy and Jimmy play what they planned. The first batter for Lions fouls twice. Sammy then lobs in a Knuckle-Curve pronator. The batter doesn't understand what is going on at all. He stands bat cocked but is unable to move against the unpredictable ball.

The ump is entirely thrown off his game, too, and calls time-out. He inspects the ball, then inspects all the balls in his bag in play for the game. He walks Jimmy up to the mound for a word with Sammy. Art comes trotting out to the middle of the diamond.

"Your pitches are not going to where they're supposed to, son," the umpire says to Sammy. "What gives?"

Art speaks up immediately and defends the pitching style as legal but tricky, even if rare in character. He suggests they get on with the game, and for anyone that doesn't understand to just go home and study. Do their homework!"

"Oh," the umpire says. "I'll be studying alright. I'll be studying that pitcher of yours, so keep yourself in line Coach Costello."

"Always, Mr. Ump." Art says with a smile.

Jimmy puts the sign down and in for a Knuckle Ball. The batter ducks and moves in fear, as the ball jumps and moves every which way, ultimately taking a called strike. Sammy throws another Knuckle Ball, just as effective, down and away. The batter gives it a swing and a miss. Jimmy signs for a pronating Cutter. Upon release, out of the right hand comes a Fastball in from the opposite side. The hitter thinks it's a

Meatball but the ball breaks hard and sudden from outside to in. A swing and a miss for strike three.

The clean-up man is up to bat for the Lions. He's a big kid and everyone knows he can hit, a known dinger. And he represents the tying run at the plate. After some mid-inning discussion, pitcher and catcher know exactly what they want to do.

Jimmy wiggles his fingers, Sammy barely nods but out of his intimidating windup comes a Foshball. The batter mistakes it for a Splitter but the ball is delivered with some tail away from the left thrown pronator with different speed.

"It's a damn dookie pitch!"

"It's a good pitch, is what it is! You just contrate on your hitting, son."

Underrated and rarely seen, everyone in

attendance blinks like the Lions players do from the dugout. The batter steps out of the box trying to somehow gather his shit.

Sammy puts a grip on for an Eephus Pitch. This pitch comes down the lane and drops on the batter to a degree that it looks like a prankster pitch. It's a custom pitch, best used on heavy hitters. It comes in thrown in the 40s. It really messes up the batter. He is visibly shaken, because he cannot cope with what he is being dealt.

In something uncharacteristic in Little League, the big batter switches sides and takes a lefty stance. The ump calls time and beckons the Lions manager over to him.

"Is this what you want to do?"

"I didn't call for it but if he thinks he can hit the damn ball from this side, so be it."

This pitch could end the inning and win the game for Kiwanis. Sammy and Jimmy want to see the batter's reaction to one of Sammy's best offerings. So, Jimmy puts a finger down, then swirls it around like he's stirring a drink at The Playboy Club.

The pronating Screwball thrown has utterly crazy movement that beat out the 3 and 2 count, just like every time it's thrown low across the plate.

Kiwanis wins again. They are the Division Leaders half way through the season.

13

Word spreads like a ground swell among the Baseball Divisions and fans for the first time in memory. They showcase an incredible pitcher-catcher pair that mop up the competition week after week. Suddenly, all those great hitters aren't looking so great anymore.

The opposing pitchers that used to dominate may still throw some boys out, most players in the Division have spent a year to rehearse batting against Fastballs and Curveballs. There is a new kid on the mound to contend with. No one can imagine the goods Jimmy and Sammy bring to the game.

People come in from out of town to watch Sammy. He has plenty of rest between games, because he averages little more than twenty-one pitches per game and has thrown more shut-outs than not. By the All-Star break, Sammy has racked up a yard full of no-hitters.

Because Kiwanis is the premier team, Manager Marusso Coaches his Division players. He decides Sammy will not start. He's got Aman and Lundquist. Aman starts and does well, striking out the first four batters he faces. Meanwhile, his offense scores four runs, most earned.

Unfortunately, the competition is warming up to Aman's heat. The base hits accomplished are quickly turning into runs scored. He walks a man home and so the catcher and Art visit the mound. The umpire is there doing what he does best, to rush everyone into doing whatever they plan to do quickly.

At one point, Art says to him, "You are quite annoying, Mr. Umpire." He raises his voice.

"Give us a G-D minute our man in blue. And that's a purely legal minute! We've got our rights and time-outs. I don't want to report you to the League."

"Geez, Art," the umpire replies, sulking. "Got to keep the game moving. It's nothing personal, it's just part of my job."

"Uh huh. I know, man."

"So, get a move on."

Art is looking over the competition roster and decides to pull Aman.

"I'm sorry Eug but I've got to pull this change. We should all have a chance to play anyway."

"I know, Coach," Eug says. "It's cool with

me." He shakes Art's hand just before walking off the mound.

The score stands at 4-2 with one out in the top of the third. Art motions for Lundquist to come in. He forgot how big this kid is!

"No matter what, throw something that moves. You can repeat pitches as you see fit but *never* repeat the location. You got that Dean?"

"Yeah Coach," Dean replies. "Got it!"

Lundquist throws a few warm-up pitches; simple Fastballs and Sliders. The umpire studies the pitcher's movements and windup. The boy is throwing hard, probably between 58 and 65 miles per hour. Dean flips his empty mitt toward the catcher letting him know he's ready as he lets go just one more.

He throws a Fastball to the third batter of this half an inning. It's a shot; a line drive directly at the 3rd baseman. Two away. The clean-up batter digs in, as the ump says, "Come on Mr. Phelps, don't ruin the grounds work."

The big lefty at the plate leans in and over as Dean winds-up. The Slider fools the batter, who takes a strike. A Fastball is dinged way over the fence but foul. The batter returns to the plate from his token four-bag trot. Art is thinking that boy is a cocky little fucker.

The count is 0 and 2. Dean knows the batter will take at least this one, so he takes a chance and serves up a Fastball that moves at the knees. Strike three and he's out, and the team is out. While Little League games are held to seven innings, the All-Star game and Championship games are played the regulation nine innings.

Art's batting order is back at the top in

the bottom of the fifth. There has yet to appear any sort of pitching threat, which makes Art believe, well, they just don't have anybody better. They have hitters, no doubt but Art's pitchers win the duals.

Two runs scored off base hits before the inning is over. Art tells Dean to start throwing that big ol' round-house curve of his. Not during the warm-up but with each batter.

"Make it your strike three pitch, buddy."

"I'll do it!" Dean is aware that's what he's known for, and what scares the pants off every batter that faces it coming at them. He's also happy to be a southpaw. So, he throws easy during the inning warm-up. He faces the bottom of the lineup who are all righties.

He sets them all up the same way. Fastball,

slider, Change-up, and then that monstrous curve, which is either missed, called or foul-ticked for the out. A perfect inning. The dugout is vibrating with the excitement of leading the All-Star game at 5-3 in the sixth.

Secret Scouting through McDowell for Cleveland and Seaver for New York are there unannounced and with tablets in hand. They don't even tell Art they are coming. Watching, they realize he is saving Sammy for the closer. Sammy's never played any role but starter, but he can't see a difference: Throw at, and strike out the batters. To him, it's just that simple.

Sammy takes the field and as he walks up to the mound he hears applause. He stops and looks briefly around. He doesn't see anybody important. He doesn't think he missed an announcement. He steps up to the mound, moves some dirt around, picks up the ball left there and gives Jimmy a chance to set himself up.

The applause fades away with a few whistles, and as Sammy turns his head slowly around to view his fielders, he notices that all eyes are on him. Every person in the stands is staring at him, smiling and clapping. He hears the spectators hoot encouragement. He looks over at his father, who gives Sammy a nod and a wink.

Sammy pitches the three final hitless innings. He and Jimmy put together sequences for each series. The general idea is to set up two strikes, then throw a specialty pitch for the strike out. They begin with either a Fastball, Slider, or perhaps a Cutter. Second pitch is a Curveball. The breadth and depth vary with each throw.

The strike out balls include Knuckle Balls,

Knuckle-Curves and that insane Screwball. The opposing Division never had a chance. Seaver and McDowell up-five each other, and Art gives Sammy a big bear hug. The team flows out of the dugout and jump around in celebration.

14

Tristy breaks her Dad's heart when she announces at the Christmas Dinner table that she is walking away from college. With just one semester to graduation, Art tries hard to change her mind and that he can't believe she could not be convinced. No one understands her reasoning. She merely repeats, "Doug and I just want to be married, and we don't want to wait."

This puts a sad and selfish, globby damper on Christmastime around the Costello table. Doug's father hands over his branch banking operations to him. So, Tristy and Doug look at the full basket before them, that blinds them to all this. And this is a thorn in Dad's side for the duration.

"You won't ever have the chance I've given you. Right now, I feel like throwing-up all over your shoes – BOTH of you!"

Doug out-does Tristy when he asks the proud Disabled American Veteran, having served thirty-years during WWII, the Korean Conflict and the Vietnam War how best to get out of the draft and avoid Basic Training and Service altogether. Art s l o w l y rises from the dinner table, visually upset, peering into Doug's eyes, says nothing, and goes to sit alone at the kitchen table.

Mom tries to hold Christmas together but sadly so, through her tears and disciplinary comments to Tristy and Doug. She decides to call for gift giving. For his own sake, she tries to leave Art out of it until he feels ready to rejoin the group.

"Sammy," Art calls for his son. "I want you to take this." Sammy can see it is an unwrapped shaving kit.

"Take this to Doug and tell him it is for him, *if he thinks he's old enough to shave!* Can you do that for me, Sam?"

Sammy gets it, so he does exactly what his Dad asks him to do, and then he walks away quickly. Art came in to challenge Doug and put him in his place; plucking his daughter out of college, attempting to dodge the draft. Art's voice is gruff, and he appears in every way quite threatening. So much so, that Tristy and Doug quickly run out of the house and speed down the five-hundred-seventy-five-foot driveway, with Tristy screaming, hanging out of the passenger side of their VW Beetle.

With Springtime right around the corner, Art procures a beautiful home just up the road from Rye Beach, near Odiorne Point, which is a peaceful destination. Given that, the area remains quiet and crime free. It's a dwelling that anybody would love to live in... on the Beach. Sammy overhears that it is a very expensive home. It is a gift for newlyweds Doug and Tristy, but Doug refuses to accept it from Art.

Another slap in Art's face. The young couple move into a small, shitty urban apartment on the second floor above a local pawn shop on the outskirts of Portsmouth. Art is through with them. Tristy walks away from her own Dad, the family, a stubborn and stuck-up brat in the name of her new husband.

TALENTS
WITH
PRACTICE

James A. Landry

15

Sammy and Jimmy begin working out two months before team practice begins. They act beyond their age on handling the fame element they walked into last year. They churned out several shut-outs and five no-hitters. The only game Sammy didn't start was the All-Star Game, but he sure finished it taking out the three hardest hitters in the opposing Division.

Sammy, Jimmy and Art agree that Sammy and Jimmy should stay the course and strive for improvements there that may present themselves. Their review includes Sammy's windup and stretch, plus the complete pitch menu. The pitcher/catcher relationship is solid, and Jimmy's pronator handling finally falls into place.

Half the Coaches in the league want very much to learn what Kiwanis's secrets are. Other brash Coaches very intentionally ignore the Phenom and arrogantly move ahead, though losing to Kiwanis along the way. This coming season, Art instructs Sammy and Jimmy to lay pronator hard and heavy. Not so much throwing nonsense to a righty or lefty but to lean toward the pronator when and where ever the opportunity arises.

They read down the menu and highlight each throw a red, yellow or green; Work, Near Perfect.

<u>Sammy's Top Best Baseball Pitches</u>

Slider; Four-Seam Fastball; Two-Seam Fastball

Curveball; Split-Finger Fastball (Splitter)

Gyroball; Screwball; Change-up

Knuckle Ball; Sinker; Cutter

Spitball; Eephus Pitch; Forkball

Foshball; Vulcan Change-up; Circle Change-up

Knuckle-Curve; Slider.

All applicable pronator throws are finally familiar enough for Jimmy to code all of them green. Sammy still needs work on his Knuckle-Curve, Eephus Pitch and Foshball: Yellow. And the rest are Green. Based on the number of balls pitched the year before, Sammy could start nearly every game, if Art so chooses but takes the rest, nice and easy and keeps Sammy passing in the bull pen.

Last year's Little League Teams graduate to Full Fledged District Teams, and Kiwanis is named Portsmouth #1. They are undefeated going into the coming season.

Team	Wins	Losses
Portsmouth#1	8	0
Concord	7	1
Portsmouth#2	6	2
Lamprey River	5	3
Rye	4	4
Somersworth	3	5
Laconia	1	7
Tilton-Northfield	1	7
Suncook	1	7

Game one pits Portsmouth#1, Home, against Portsmouth#2, Away. PoTown-1 acquired Dean Lundquist in the off-season, and PoTown-2 drafted Eug Aman. The Coaches hold their pre-game lineup and roster walk-thru with the home plate umpire. Sammy starts for PoTown-1, and Eug starts for PoTown-2.

Pitching sequences have already been noted by Sammy and Jimmy. Sammy has the reminders film-taped to his left arm and Jimmy has his duct taped to the back of his glove. This causes the umpire to take notice and investigate. He learns they're nothing more than a set list of cliff-notes and strolls back behind the plate.

"Cliff Notes. . .Hmmm," he says to himself.

"PLAY BALL!" He bellows.

Sammy winds up and throws a Slider, swung on and missed. He pitches a strong Gyroball. The batter stood still mesmerized for a called strike two. Jimmy calls for a Knuckle-Curve. This ball appears to have come from the sky and jumped past the batter for strike three.

PoTown-1 comes up to bat after practicing over half their training for Aman's Fastball. The first batter goes down swinging. The second batter singles into right field. The third batter gets tricked by a Breaking Ball. Big Jay Barfield steps into the batter's box and scratches a takeoff point in the dirt.

"Take it easy there, Barfield." The umpire says. Jay doesn't hear, therefore doesn't know, and clearly does not care.

Barfield takes a Fastball right down the lane, if not a little low.

"Nope! *Ball!* Low!" The umpire announces emphatically.

Aman wings a hard, fast breaking ball. Barfield takes it for a strike. Aman is convinced he's got Barfield. He pitches a slow Curveball. Barfield waits for the downward movement. It never comes. And there it is. The meatball that Barfield swings at, connects and hits. It's a line drive homerun, scoring two. Batter five grounds out on a lame Fastball.

The score holds at 2-0 for five innings. Art decides to relieve Sammy with Dean. There is nothing that tells Art that the players are any less scared of the big left-hander. Art has him sequence with back-to-back roundhouse curveballs changing locations. His first pitch in the sequence is a Cutter he's been practicing during the off-season.

Dean dominates the final two innings, saves the game and is celebrated by his new team like he never has before. What a great feeling. . .being wanted. . .being appreciated. He's been taken advantage of all his life; at home, at school and even in Baseball.

WHAT A
BIG HIT

16

Sammy starts the All-Star Game full of confidence. He and Jimmy have pitch sequences down pat and worked out how to change any sign at any time, as Jimmy, or either of them feel fit or necessary. Art has all the Division leaders, which includes a sharp pitching bull pen. He has Aman, Lundquist and three others who were voted into the All-Stars.

Jimmy has Sammy toss a traditional sequence; Fastball, Curveball and Change of Pace. There are two men on, and Jimmy makes a change. The new sequences are Curveball, Splitter, then Gyroball; Screwball, Change-up, Eephus

Pitch, and then Knuckle Ball; Sinker, and Cutter.

These pitches, especially with Sammy's speed and his ability to throw exquisite Change-ups mow down the competitors one after another.

"Nice job adjusting you guys." Art says to his pitcher and catcher.

The hitting suffers today, which makes him doubly grateful for a great pitching staff. Barfield gets on twice but gets stranded, however he also dings a three-run homer in the eighth. Going into the last inning, Sammy stands for the last time today on the All-Star mound.

He strikes out the first batter in the lineup. He stands quiet and still while waiting for the pinch hitter to prepare then step into the batter's box. The batter is not a starter but stands at about six feet tall and overweight, probably nearing 245 pounds. Yes, Sammy thinks, yeah, he is intimidating.

Sammy plans on pronator pitches to this guy; some tricky stuff. No Fastballs - even his movers and shakers. Jimmy and he decide on a pronator round-house Curveball. The batter takes it for a strike. Sammy throws a wicked Cutter. The batter swings and misses.

There seems to be a quiet pause all around him, and Sammy steps back, takes a deep breath and has a look around the park. People are on their feet. He sees the cheering but barely hears it. It is for him, but he pays no attention and does not feel distracted at all.

Art, McDowell and Seaver taught him well. He steps forward enough to barely toe the rubber. He swipes at it with his cleats. He knows what he's about to throw at the big batter, who is squared and ready.

Sammy takes his full windup and delivers a Knuckle-Curve. Jimmy reaches high as the ball refuses to drop. The batter looks like ol' Frank Howard as he takes a flashing quick swing. A loud crack echoes through the small stadium. The bat breaks and flies twirling toward third base. The coach there catches the fat end, looks at it and throws it down to the ground.

Sammy immediately collapses on the mound. He is starched. Starched. He already has a Baseball-sized knot just above his left temple and he is out cold. He is lifeless.

The batter begins to run toward first base but once there stands still, as ordered by his first base Coach. There is a small crowd surrounding Sammy. Art calls for space. The paramedics on scene are right there.

They confirm that Sammy is unconscious but alive. . .yet barely so.

Art and the Coaches, Jimmy and the team are in tears and completely in fear. The gurney wheels Sammy into the back of the ambulance. Art travels with Sammy in the back. The medics take vitals and try in vain to wake the young man up. The pulse is slow. The breathing is shallow, and he is put on a Respiratory Breathing Pump. Every three pumps he flatlines for two.

The game is called given the circumstances and given to Marusso and Costello. Jimmy sits in the dugout repeatedly uttering the words, "Fucking Meatball. . .Fucking Meatball. . .Fucking Meatball. . ."

The game ball is wedged into the side of Sammy's head. It sticks out like a rock in a retainer wall. It's encircled with thin strands of blood and hair. Sammy's eyes are barely open but there is no sign of life. The ball falls out and rolls a few inches when the medic sprays the wound with Betadine. Sammy's head is now swelling rapidly and bleeding rather profusely.

Art picks up the ball and looks at it like it will tell him something. He massages it and squeezes it. He swears he can feel a flat spot where it slammed into Sammy's skull, which immediately sprouts a Baseball-sized tumor of sorts where the ball had been.

At the hospital, the ER doctor drains a few ounces of blood from the wound. Unimanually, in such a short period, the knot on the side of Sammy's head is hard as a rock.

Slipping below the stats in the EMT van, there is no sign of life. Throughout the evening, the respirator is secured and noisy, a feeding tube is inserted, a catheter put into place, and the vitals monitors are double-checked along with the IV drips and saline solution. The ER doctor has Sammy on an operating table. His surgical team works quickly but precisely on Sammy's head, both inside the skull and out.

The nurse explains the IV Drip bag is held higher than the patient's head, and a needle with a tube on the end of it is inserted into a patient's vein somewhere in the arm. The tube is kept stationary by film-taping it to the arm. The intravenous solution is stored in a plastic bag and distributed through a plastic tube. She is trying to distract the Costellos from the tragedy. Art appreciates knowing what is going on.

The amount of fluid entering the body is regulated through a pump or a valve in the tube. It is explained that this indicates treatment for dehydration, depending on the severity of each case. The dosage of intravenous sodium chloride changes based on a person's weight, age, medical condition and response to treatment, per the senior Attendant.

Doctors may also use a saline drip to deliver other injectable medications. Although hospitals most commonly use intravenous sodium chloride solutions, clinics and doctor's offices may also have these medications available for patients. The ER doctor comes into the waiting room.

"Mr. Costello," the doctor begins. "I want to give to you an informational packet to educate you thoroughly about head injury, first aid and beyond. Please remain patient. Your son is receiving the best care available. A head injury is any trauma to the scalp, skull, or brain. The injury may be only a minor bump on the skull or a serious brain injury. And with head injury, it can be either closed or open, such as penetrating. Please take the time to read this info pack and share it. It is considered mandatory reading for you in this case, sir. May I count on that?"

"Yes doctor, I'll read it through. Thank you."

"A closed head injury means you receive a hard blow to the head from striking an object, but the object does not break the skull. That appeared to be what happened with your loved one, however, upon closer and clearer observation, he does indeed appear to have a fractured skull.

"An open, or penetrating head injury means you are hit with an object that breaks the skull and enters the brain. This is more likely to happen when you move at high speed, such as going through the windshield during

a car accident. It can also happen from a gunshot to the head."

Art goes to the Chapel, sits in front of the Mother Mary candelabra and reads on.

"Head injuries include concussion, in which the brain is shaken, and is the most common type of traumatic brain injury. Scalp wounds, skull fractures and head injuries may cause bleeding in the brain tissue. Within the layers that surround the brain you may read or hear these mentioned: subarachnoid hemorrhage, subdural hematoma or extradural hematoma.

"Head injury is a common reason for an emergency room visit. Many people who suffer head injuries are children. Traumatic brain injury accounts for over 1 in 6 injury related hospital admissions each year. Common causes of head injury include: Accidents at home, *work, outdoors, or while playing sports, falls, physical assault and traffic accidents."*

Art is reading fast.

"Most of these injuries are minor because the skull protects the brain. Some injuries are severe enough to require a stay in the hospital.

"Some Symptoms: head injuries may cause bleeding in the brain tissue and the layers that surround the brain. Symptoms of a head injury can occur right away, or symptoms can develop slowly over several hours or days. Even if the skull is not fractured, the brain can hit the inside of the skull and be bruised. The head may look fine, but problems could result from bleeding or swelling inside the skull.

"The spinal cord is also likely to be injured in any serious trauma.

"Some head injuries cause changes in brain function. This is called a traumatic brain injury. A concussion is a mild traumatic brain injury. Symptoms of a concussion can range from mild to severe.

"First Aid in that case: Learning to recognize a serious head injury and give basic first aid can save someone's life. For a moderate to severe head injury, we urge people to call 911 and report the crises right away.

"Get medical help right away if the person becomes very sleepy, behaves abnormally, develops a severe headache or stiff neck. The pupils sometimes are of unequal sizes. The patient is unable to move an arm or leg. A loss of consciousness, even briefly, should immediately be attended to. If the fallen person vomits more than once, bring him to the ER or call for ambulatory care. These are all indications of head injury. If any of them apply, take the following steps:

"Check the person's airway, breathing, and circulation. If necessary, begin rescue breathing and CPR.

"If the person's breathing and heart rate are normal but the person is unconscious, we will check and treat as if there is a spinal injury. Stabilize the head and neck by placing your hands on both sides of the person's head. Keep the head in line with the spine and prevent movement. Wait for medical help.

"Stop any bleeding by firmly pressing a clean cloth on the wound. If the injury is serious be careful not to move the person's head. If blood soaks through the cloth do not remove it. Place another cloth over the first one.

"If you suspect a skull fracture, do not apply direct pressure to the bleeding site, and do not remove any debris from the wound. Cover the wound with sterile gauze dressing.

"If the person is vomiting, to prevent choking roll the person's head, neck, and body as one unit onto their side. This still protects the spine, which you must always assume is injured in the case of a head injury. Children often vomit once after a head injury. This may not be a problem but call a doctor right away for further guidance. Once at the hospital, the ER nurse applies ice packs to swollen areas.

"Follow these precautions, some 'Do Nots':

"Do NOT wash a head wound that is deep or bleeding a lot.

"Do NOT remove any object sticking out of a wound.

"DO NOT move the person unless absolutely necessary.

"DO NOT shake the person if he or she seems dazed.

"DO NOT remove a helmet if you suspect a serious head injury.

"DO NOT pick up a fallen child with any sign of head injury.

"DO NOT drink alcohol within 48 hours of a serious head injury.

"A serious head injury that involves bleeding or brain damage must be treated in a hospital.

"For a mild head injury, no treatment may be needed. However, watch for symptoms of a head injury, which can show up later.

"Your health care provider will explain what to expect, how to manage any headaches, how to treat other symptoms. You will be notified when the patient is cleared to return to sports, school, work, and other activities. There are signs or symptoms to worry about.

"Children will need to be watched and make activity changes.

"Adults also need close observation and activity changes.

"Both adults and children must follow the providers', that is the medical team, instructions about when it will be possible to return to athletics, sports and so on.

"So, when do you contact a Medical Professional?

"Call 911 right away if:

"There is severe head or face bleeding.

"The person is confused, tired, or unconscious.

"The person stops breathing.

"You suspect a serious head or neck injury, or the person develops any signs or symptoms of a serious head injury.

"Expect tests and diagnosis and further appointments & care.

"We take the time to listen, to find answers and to provide you the best care.

"Learn more. Request an appointment.

"Because traumatic brain injuries are usually emergencies and because consequences can worsen swiftly without treatment, doctors usually need to assess the situation rapidly."

An ER Physician's Assistant tells Art, "Glasgow Coma Scale is being administered to your boy, Mr. Costello. This 15-point test helps doctors and other emergency medical personnel to assess the initial severity of a brain injury by checking a person's ability to follow directions and move their eyes and limbs. The coherence of speech also provides important clues. Abilities are scored numerically in the Glasgow Coma Scale. Higher scores mean less severe injuries."

Art returns to the packet and resumes reading:

"'*Information about the injury and symptoms*':

"*If you observe someone being injured or arrive immediately after an injury, you may be able to provide medical personnel with information that's useful in assessing the injured person's condition.*

"*Answers to the following questions may be beneficial in judging the severity of injury:*

"*How did the injury occur?*

"*Did the person lose consciousness?*

"How long was the person unconscious?

"Did you observe any other changes in alertness, speaking, coordination or other signs of injury?

"Where was the head or other parts of the body struck?

"Can you provide any information about the force of the injury? For example, what hit the person's head, how far did he or she fall, or was the person thrown from a vehicle?

"Was the person's body whipped around or severely jarred?

**Note that Imaging Tests will certainly be performed.*

"A Computerized Tomography (CT) scan will be administered. A CT scan uses a series of X-rays to create a detailed view of the brain. A CT scan can quickly visualize fractures and

uncover evidence of bleeding in the brain, a hemorrhage, blood clots or hematomas, bruised brain tissue or contusions and brain tissue swelling.

"A Magnetic Resonance Imaging (MRI) may be performed. An MRI uses powerful radio waves and magnets to create a detailed view of the brain. This test may be used after the person's condition has been stabilized.

"Intracranial pressure monitoring is a must.

"Tissue swelling from a traumatic brain injury can increase pressure inside the skull and cause additional damage to the brain. Doctors may insert a probe through the skull to monitor this pressure."

"I know that was a lot to take in, sir but

I need you to be in the know with your boy, the nurse's activities and what the doctors are doing during the trauma. Just because the doctors, at times, aren't as visible as the nurses and attendants, does not mean we have abandoned you. We are working non-stop in our own work spaces, running and analyzing test results, and so on."

17

Art, Sophia and the girls doze off and on throughout the night. Early morning comes with the stark reality that it isn't a dream. The ECU doctor gently wakes Art and walks him down the hall.

"I know what you or most people think about when you hear the word coma. A coma can be difficult to understand, especially because people sometimes jokingly use the word coma to describe people who are sleeping deeply or not paying attention. But a coma is a serious condition that has nothing to do with sleep. So, what happens when someone is in a coma?

"Someone who is in a coma is unconscious and will not respond to voices, other sounds, or any sort of activity going on nearby. The person is still alive, but the brain is functioning at its lowest stage of alertness. We can't shake and wake up someone who is in a coma like you can someone who has just fallen asleep. Mr. Costello, Sammy is in a coma. Are we clear?"

"What can cause a coma?" Art wants to know more.

"Comas can be caused by different things, including a severe injury to the head that hurts the brain, seizures, infections involving the brain, brain damage caused by a lack of oxygen for too long, an overdose of medicine or other drugs, a stroke and chemical imbalances, such as those in the body from other illnesses.

"When one of these things happens, it

can mess up how the brain's cells work. This can hurt the parts of the brain that make someone conscious, and if those parts stop working, the person will stay unconscious."

"How do people take care of someone in a coma?"

"Someone in a coma usually needs to be cared for in the intensive care unit of the hospital. There, the person can get extra care and attention from doctors, nurses, and other hospital staff. They make sure the person gets fluids, nutrients, and any medicines needed to keep the body as healthy as possible. These are sometimes given through a tiny plastic tube inserted in a vein or through a feeding tube that brings fluids and nutrients directly to the stomach.

"Some comatose people are unable to breathe on their own and need the help of a ventilator, a machine that pumps air into the lungs through a tube placed in the windpipe. The hospital staff also tries to prevent bedsores in someone who is comatose. Bedsores are open sores on the body that come from lying in one place for too long without moving at all.

"It can be very upsetting and frustrating for a person's family to see someone they love in a coma, and they may feel scared and helpless. But they can help take care of the person. Taking time to visit the hospital and read to, talk to, and even play music for the patient are important because it's possible that the person may be able to hear what's going on, even if he or she cannot respond."

"What happens after a coma?"

"Usually, a coma does not last more than a few weeks. Sometimes, however, a person stays in a coma for a longer time -- even months or years -- and will be able to do very little except breath on his or her own.

"Most people do come out of comas and some of them can return to the normal lives they had before they got sick.

"On TV, it seems like someone in a coma wakes up right away, looks around, and is able to think and talk normally. But in real life, this rarely happens. When coming out of a coma, a person probably will be confused and only slowly respond to what's going on. It will take time for the person to start feeling better.

"Whether someone fully returns to normal after being in a coma depends on what caused the coma and how badly the brain may have been damaged. Sometimes people who come out of comas are just as they were before. They can remember what happened to them before the coma and can do everything they used to do. That is the most or the best you can hope and pray for.

"Other people may need therapy to relearn basic things like tying their shoes, eating with a fork or spoon, or learning to walk all over again. They also may have problems with speaking or remembering things.

"Over time and with the help of therapists, however, many people who have been in a coma can make a lot of progress. They may not be exactly like they were before the coma, but they can do many things and enjoy life with their family and friends. You and your family should try and stay rested, optimistic and calm."

"Thank you, Doctor."

18

Sammy remains comatose going on six weeks. The best sign to his family is the rosy color in his cheeks, and the warmth of his skin. Either parent, sometimes both together and occasionally the girls, typically one or the other regularly pay visits, short as they may sometimes be.

Sophia feels so sorry for Art, who has fallen into a deep depression. He refuses the psychiatrist and the meds offered. He does, however, see a behavioral therapist once a week. Most therapists cannot write prescriptions but offer talk therapy the breadth and depth of which Art could never have imagined. It helps.

As Art walks by the mantle, he notices his Service Award pen in pieces, with a broken, maple stand as well.

"Girls! Girls!" He calls down the hallway.

"Coming, Dad," Tristy hollers back.

"Where's Anita?" His voice is still raised.

Sophia has seen the broken pen set but says nothing. She remains aphonic and hushed as the girls bound into the living room. She is not conditioned to reticence or suppression, but she does know when to butt out. Nothing good, she feels, can come from this.

"Who broke my award pen?" Art demands to know, in a voice just a hair louder than a man in a confessional. His disposition and presence are clearly not the same demeaner since Sammy's accident on the field.

"Who. . .broke. . .my. . .FUCKING PEN? I said." The girls think he is turning into The Shining's Jack Torrance, and they are scared.

Again, that is one of the few times the 'F' word has ever been uttered in the Costello home, and it scares everyone there out of their shoes. All go silent. Dad wants to know. He must know. It is today's obsession.

"Anita?" Art asks calmly. "Did you do this?"

"No, Daddy. I swear I did not ruin your pen. I swear to God. I did not touch your pen. I never even touched it since the day you came home with it and showed it to us."

Anita is crying the sad tears of a young teenager. Sophia comes to the living room and slowly, gently walks Anita the kitchen. They sit and calmly sip tea and pick at buttered raspberry scones.

"Guess what," Art says to Tristy while poking her left collar bone. *"You're it!"*

"Daddy," Tristy uses her most pitiful whimper and the reference to her Dad she knows he likes the most. "I didn't do it. Why would I take a pen apart at my age?"

"You girls never cease to amaze me! That's why!

"If the threaded end pieces were not broken, I may have had a chance to fix it. But not now. . .Look at this! It looks like they were chewed on by an infant. . .or an animal!"

Tristy ruses a few seconds and takes a wager in jeopardy. "Well, maybe Sammy did it." She deadpans. Art turns beet red.

"Don't you *ever* mention my son's name. Especially when he is lying unconscious in a hospital bed! And don't you *ever* imply anything about anybody not present to defend themselves!"

"OK Daddy. OK," Tristy says on the verge of tears. "I'm sorry. I'm really sorry."

She walks quickly into the kitchen where all three females of the house are trying to stifle their cries.

Even without Sammy, Kiwanis has a winning season but loses during the play-offs. They decide to wear their hats in the dugout inside out, otherwise in silence as a tribute and a prayer to Sammy. The relief and closers keep their hats turned inside out and so do the 2nd string players.

Art stops wearing a cap altogether. He feels like everything he does could somehow bounce back to Sammy. He doesn't want to display any flavor of what could in any way be contemplated blasphemy. As usual he heads over to the hospital to sit next to his son.

He finds Sophia there with her rosary beads woven among her fingers. He greets her with a kiss and hug. Sammy's eyes are slits. The lids are open enough for a peek. But they both see there is no one there. It is an eerie sight. Art must remind himself repeatedly that Sammy is *not* a dead young man, and the eye lids are part of his symptoms. His limbs and digits are soft and pliable, not stiff at all. This pleases Sophia, who says. "Feel his hand and his arm Art."

He's nice and warm.

19

Art has a court date in Hartford, Connecticut. He's fighting a speeding ticket a trooper wrote him up for on his way to Shae Stadium last month. He and Sophia travel without the kids this time.

They arrive back in Portsmouth, and on the way home, they pick-up Tristy and Anita, who spent the past few days on a visit with Grampy. Dad's Dad. Tristy's friends met her there and picked her up for a weekend over-nighter and an outing to the beach.

Art and Sophia immediately go to the hospital to check on Sammy. They beckon for

Anita to come but in a broken, cracking voice from inside her room she declines. As soon as she hears the car pull away, Anita begins weeping in her room. Fortunately, Tristy isn't home to make fun of her.

Anita hears in mind his words in repetition. "And don't you dare mention a word of this to anyone. Do you understand, little girl? I will tell them you're a liar. Who do you think they are going to believe? Some cranky little girl, or good old Grampy? Heh? You don't want to hurt your Dad and Mom, do you? Not a word, you little slut! Not one word!"

Anita is still in her room when her parents arrive home. She is whimpering and hyperventilating. Her Mom calls softly through the door: "Anita, baby, are you alright?"

"Um, no Mom. I am not alright."

"Please open the door and talk to me, dear. You'll feel much better."

"Mom, he said he'd kill us all."

"Who said that? Your Grampy said that?"

"Yes, Mom."

"Tell me what else he's been doing."

"I can't. I can't. It's awful."

"Anita," Mom says. "Nothing is worse than not knowing. I can help you. Daddy will help you. Our whole family will be right behind you. Please tell me what Grampy has been doing to you."

"It's not just me. I've seen him lead Sammy down the cellar stairs too.

"He sticks his finger in my vagina. . .in and out; in and out. It hurts."

"What else?"

"He does the same thing in my rear end hole. I saw him do that to Sammy, too."

Art is further than beside himself. He is on fire. What the hell should he do? He doesn't want to put his kids through court. Perhaps he can film their testimony and deliver it by proxy. He is steaming inside and wants nothing less than to break his father's door down and confront the old man.

This explains the reluctance of Anita and Sammy to go and visit Grampy. Art completely believes his kids. They have no reason to bring anything like this up ad hoc. When he asks Tristy, she says he has never touched her that she can remember, but she has opted to sleep over friends' houses mostly instead of staying at Grampy's.

"Jeezum Crow, Sophia,' Art begins. "We've

got Sammy laying in a coma at the hospital, and now these accusations from Anita?"

"These are more than accusations, Mister Art Costello!" Sophia says sharply. "These are truths of the matter. *TABERNACLE, Art, Anita is telling the truth!*" Art has never heard Sophia curse like that in French *or* English.

Art drives over to Gosling Meadows and parks in front of his father's house. He slams the car door behind him. He walks fast to the back door, which is usually open. He crashes through the screen door and sees Grammy Laura in the kitchen corner, eating a Fig Newton.

"Get the fuck upstairs now, ma. *Now!* Get the fuck up there!"

Art rounds the corner into the dim TV room. His father is pissing into an old coffee can.

The moment he finishes, Art charges him and knocks him back into his decrepit old tweed recliner.

"Tell me what you've been doing to my kids!"

"Nothing. What is wrong with you?"

"You old lying sack of shit. You've been fingering Anita. . .*and* Sammy!"

"You don't understand, Art."

"Make me understand you stinking piece of rubbish!"

"They like it. . .We like it."

"Get ready to die you motherfuckin' cocksucker!" These words Art has never uttered, even under his breath.

Art grabs a pillow from the couch and lunges at his father. He holds the pillow over the old man's face and puts down a cracking neck-hold until well after his father's legs stop shaking and kicking. It doesn't take long in the kind of shape the elderly man is in.

"Die motherfucker, die!"

"Laura, ma,'" Art yells up the stairs to his step mother. "There is something wrong with Dad. We ought to check it out." He speeds away in his black Ford Falcon.

Anita is enrolled in therapy to soften the blows she's been through. She goes twice a week and tells her parents that she likes it. "The people there are so nice," she says. "They all seem to understand. And they all seem to want to help."

"Anita darling," Art asks. "Why did you

wait until Sammy got hurt before saying anything?"

"Because I couldn't stand it anymore. And Sammy has been getting all this attention, all this time."

Art whispers into Sophia's ear, "Is this what they call 'middle child syndrome?'"

"Take that to the therapist, won't you, please? Good Lord!

"Oh, and by the way, Anita admits that Tristy's boyfriend took the award pen apart and broke it. There, you have it."

"Oh, is that right," Art replies. "Thank you for clearing that up for me, darling. . .Anita."

And Sophia adds, "Don't worry, we won't mention your name."

In a group hug, Mom and Dad assure Anita that her nightmares are over, and she'll never have to face that distressing, gruesome old man ever again. Tristy walks in the front door and knows right away that something is very wrong. She can smell the tears.

20

Art reads his way through the laminate brochure in the folder given him by the surgeon over four months ago.

'The Coma is common with severe brain injuries, especially injuries that affect the arousal center in the brain stem. Understanding a coma can be difficult because there are many levels of coma. In general, coma is a lack of awareness of one's self and what is around the injured. A person in a coma can't sense or respond to the needs of his body or his environment.' Art reads.

'Typically, a person in a coma:

'*May or may not have their eyes closed all the time.*

'*Cannot communicate.*

'*Cannot move in a purposeful way, such as following instructions like "squeeze my hand," or "open your eyes."*

Because their eyes may be closed, many of us think of someone in a coma as being asleep. The difference is that you can get someone to open their eyes when they are asleep. But you can't get someone in a coma to open their eyes otherwise. Their eyes are closed because the normal sleeping and waking pattern has been disrupted. Many times, the eyes are taped shut to protect them from injury and drying out.

They cannot follow directions or communicate because their brain doesn't process information the way it used to. It is also common for breathing and blood pressure to be affected. If so, proper care will be needed to help control breathing or blood pressure for them.

There is no set pattern of recovery from coma but there are signs that may mean improvement in coming out of a coma. Signs of coming out of a coma include being able to keep their eyes open for longer and longer periods of time and being awakened from 'sleep' easier at first by pain such as a pinch, then by touch like gently shaking of their shoulder and finally by sound, like calling their name.

"Emerging from Coma and Signs of Improvement." Art reads on.

Oh, how Art longs for the day, and asks the Lord from deep inside, "How much longer, Heavenly Father?"

Not everyone who has a brain injury emerges from a coma. If they do, they may follow a common pattern. Emerging from a coma is not like waking up from regular sleep.

When your loved one first starts to 'wake up' from or come out of the coma, he may not be able to focus his eyes. He may or may not be able to respond to you. He may look as if he is staring off into space. Part of this is from the injury or part of it may be from medicine. Movement can be another sign of improvement. At first, movements may be random like flailing arms, then may progress to semi-purposeful, such as pulling at tubes and possibly moving in response to instructions, such as "Squeeze my hand." The patient's awareness of self and his surroundings increases as he improves and gets better.

Visual and auditory tracking is another

sign of improvement. Following sights and sounds are promising signs. Tracking is when your loved one watches you as you move around the room or turns their head toward you when they see you or hear your voice.

The next stage of improvement is when your loved one begins to follow some commands intermittently even and is also consistently tracking sights and sounds. Following commands intermittently means they won't 'squeeze your hand' every time you ask. As they get better, they will follow commands more regularly.

21

Art sits by his son's bed as he does nearly every night. He dozes off and on with the imaginative play in his own mind but wakes to inanimation every time he does. Sophia relieves him in the wee hours of the morning. Watching and waiting comes wrapped around the rest of the days coming on and all that entails.

Anita and Tristy go for the late afternoon visit. It is Sammy's birthday, and his room is overfilled with flowers, candy, toys, cards, autographed bats, mitts and baseballs. Art takes photos of everything. Sammy's attendants are ordered to clear the room at the end of the day. They keep everything best they can for him in the smaller, near-empty room next door.

Anita has a hold on Sammy's left hand, while Tristy keeps some distance, without touching. Anita asks her, "Why won't you hold his hand or touch him?"

"Don't you get it, Anita?" Tristy sounds testy. "There's nothing there. That isn't Sammy. That's a humanoid body encasement wrapped all around nothing. His soul left him at the ball field."

"Oh, my god, Tristy, have you no compassion for, and an affinity to our own little brother? I mean, *God!*" And for the first time ever, Anita slaps Tristy hard across the mouth.

"Leave me alone little sister." Tristy growls.

"Yeah. I'll leave you alone and so will Jesus when your time comes."

"I'll leave that till when I'm at the Gates. Shut up!"

"Why are you even *here?*" Anita asks cynically, kicking her chair behind her. Tristy stands up, flips Anita the bird and says, "I'm not!" And walks out.

Art and Sophia show-up around four o'clock in the afternoon. They both give Anita a kiss on the forehead. She suddenly wakes, startled.

"It's just us, honey," Mom says.

Anita looks up at her father, and slowly begins to leak tears.

"Are you alright, Anita?"

"Um, yes," She answers. Then she blurts "Daddy!"

"What is it sweetheart?"

"I feel something in Sammy's hand."

"Are you sure?"

"Yes, Dad, yes!"

Art looks down, takes hold of Sammy's right hand, and then he looks into his son's squinted eyes.

"Sophia, push the orange button then go to the hall and hail an attendant! Hurry, now!"

Sammy's hands seem to be throbbing or tightening slightly, and his eyes are twitching, darting around the room. Sometimes just one at a time. Three doctors and five nurses show-up as if in queue. The nurses test the muscle movement in the hands but further, slowly, gently run their fingers over his body; his arms, torso, legs feet and hands.

"May I ask the family to please step outside for just a short while?"

"Of course, doctor," Art says. "Come on out with me ladies."

"Sammy. Sammy," the lead surgeon speaks close to the ear with his voice, soft and low and calming. "Don't force yourself to do or say anything. If you can easily respond, then please do.

"I just have a few questions for you, for now, and then we'll have you rest. OK? So, what is the memory you most connect with right now?"

"Fucking Meatball. . . Fucking Meatball. . . Fucking Meatball!"

"Meatball, Sammy?"

"I hung a Knuckle-Curve a little too high for too long against a big hitter. He ate the meatball but not for a homer. I saw the bat fly down the third base line and then I lost it. I caught a half a second of a fucking meatball coming at me and went down to sleep before I hit the ground."

Sammy, exhausted, falls back into repose but not before giving Anita, Sophia and Art a squeeze. The doctor asks if anyone knows what a "fucking meatball" is.

"He repeats it three times and appears frustrated."

Art speaks up. "Baseball pitchers that hang a Curveball too high before breaking call it a 'meatball.' It simply means that a big hungry batter at the plate will never turn way from a meatball. It's like one on a plate of pasta, typically he'll ding it over the outfield wall."

"This may be the most impressive coma recovery I've ever witnessed in person. His memory of the accident is spot on. He remembers seeing the broken bat helicopter down the third base line but moreover, he recognized his pitch and the ball reaching his head!"

"Not common, I take it."

"Not at all Mr. Costello."

22

Art calls McDowell and Seaver to let them know Sammy is coming out of it. He's getting stronger every day, eating more and calls to be more active. He can't stand waiting for that freakin' physical therapist! At least someone from the family is there with him during the afternoon and evening.

Sammy calls a nurse. "Hey nurse, may I please have a baseball?

"We have no baseballs here, Sammy. I'm sorry." She does not think about his birthday gifts stored away.

"Call my Dad and ask him to bring one to me. Please? Can you do that for me?"

"I'll give him a call, Sammy."

"Oh great. . .thank you very much."

"It's no problem at all, pal."

Art and Sammy consult with the physical therapist, coaching him on exactly what Sammy must get back into play shape. Of course, they start from the bottom up. His legs and feet are weak. His core is soft. His arms are loose, and his grip feels like he's starting all over again.

He works out every day, sometimes switching muscle mass groups from one day to the next. His therapist really does know how to mix it up. Sammy is happy with him. That automatically makes Art happy too. Sammy will remain at the rehab facility for another ninety days before going home and practicing in the alley. It's all he and Jimmy talk about.

"Hey Jimmy, I'm getting my grips back," Sammy says. "I do the full rotation a dozen times a day."

"So, like, Sammy," Jimmy begins. "How is your head, man? I mean you took a fucking big hit!"

"Well, they've removed what didn't belong there. They've installed a drain in case fluid builds up and the last thing they're going to do, is embed a steel plate in my head to protect the location of the wound."

"Holy shit, dude. How do you feel about playing? Are you a little bit scared?"

"Naw, Jimmy. No more afraid than I was when I first started in peewee league."

They share a hearty laugh, sit back, and chill.

Sammy's folks arrive just as Jimmy is leaving. They can't get over how good and strong their boy looks.

"Well, Mom, they feed me three times a day, plus snacks, and Dad, I get a heck of a workout every day."

Sammy spends the remainder of the sentient visit quiet but conscious. Babe Ruth league is about to start-up with drafts, picks, trades and walk-ons. Sammy is known around the ball fields as "the kid that made it."

"The boy was pronounced dead twice during the whole ordeal last year."

No one has seen him pitch since last year but if confidence and determination have anything to do with it, he looks ready. Due to technicalities, he must be introduced as a walk-on. People stand and cheer for him at least five or six minutes. He tips his cap and briefly waves, out of a shared respect.

Although Kiwanis wants him back, they'd have to win the players lottery to get him. Unfortunately for them, Moose puts every single token they have in the jar for Sammy. Moose is the current league champs and have been, on and off for seven seasons. There's not much they need but to have a quest, it is for pitching. Sammy and Jimmy receive congratulations, and the coveted maroon trimmed Moose uniform and warm-up jacket.

There are seven weeks to practice before the first game. Jimmy, who comes as a package with Sammy, have Art, McDowell and Seaver coach the boys relentlessly. All of them want the full menu back in-play. When asked how he felt about that Knuckle-Curve, Sammy shakes it off and says simply, "I'll *never* make the same mistake twice."

His cohorts five, knuckle and slap each other with their caps.

"Hey Jimmy," Art calls. "Sit down here with us and tell us what you're seeing and feeling with Sammy's performance. Pitch by pitch, spill your guts."

23

The wind up, stretch and delivery are perfectly executed. Sammy hasn't lost a thing. The pitches come impeccably, one after another. He changes pitching sequence and location beautifully. His small audience looks on in awe, leaning toward disbelief.

"Has anyone in Athletics mentioned your wound?" Art asks. "Have they offered you anything? You know. . .to help protect you?"

"Well, first off, I have a titanium plate covering the entire wound site and more. What they suggested was for me to wear a batting helmet while pitching."

"Oh yeah?" McDowell says.

"I politely rejected the idea but told them that I'd keep it in mind."

"Good boy, Sammy." Art is proud of his son. "As long as it is a suggestion, alright, and not a Release Order."

All eyes are on Sammy and Jimmy when they report to their first team practice. No one really knows the power that lay just below the surface but of course they've heard the rumors, and some faced him in Little League. Small cliques form on the diamond and Jimmy swears he can hear what they're saying. He and Sammy just look at each other and wait for their names to be called.

"And finally, I'd like to introduce Sammy Costello and Jimmy Presta, who are both walk-ons. As you may recall, beyond the incredible pitching record over the last two years,

Sammy took a line drive to the head. He was unconscious for months but obviously, eventually woke from his coma. He's been practicing with Jimmy, his exclusive catcher here, for several months.

"And they have been training under the tutoring of none other than Sam 'The Man' McDowell and New York Mets superstar Tom Seaver. They, along with Coach Art Costello have made the call that Sammy is ready to play ball again."

The League Coaches begin an applause that spills over the bleachers, and the entire Moose team. Most clap, some ignore, as Moose is known to be the cockiest Division League team.

The Coach writes notes on a legal-size Steno Pad.

"Please form a walk-through gauntlet to

greet them, and you might just get another surprise for your very own!"

The team offers high fives, low fives, knuckle busters and pats on the back. Most utter niceties, like "Welcome" or "Good to have you."

As each player meets the two young stars, he is handed a box. Inside are two smaller boxes. Kids get excited when they see gifts, but these boys wait until the meet and greet is over, and for the okay from their head Coach before opening them.

As the team flings the packaging to the ground, the exclamations can be heard everywhere. Sam McDowell and Tom Seaver did Sammy and Art a big one by delivering for every Moose player a brand-new baseball in its own transparent globe on a wooden stand. What's more are the autographs of every starting team player for Sam McDowell's '67

Cleveland Indians, and the other, a ball signed by Tom Seaver and the entire starting lineup of the '68 New York Mets.

"Now, you guys know our new teammates wanted to gift you these balls, it was their idea, but it is the spirit of Sam McDowell, Tom Seaver and the spirit of Baseball itself that made it happen. So, let's clean-up the litter, stash your goods and run a few laps."

Art walks over to Coach Dunfeld, smiles, and says softly, "It's all about delivery, eh, Coach?"

". . .And timing, just like a good comedian!"

They laugh together.

24

"If there is any doubt lingering around our new man Sammy's talent, we're going to play a little game." As he speaks, Sammy takes his place on the mound and Jimmy, his, behind the plate.

"The rest of the team will face them via the batters on-deck circle. You'll get nine pitches coming your way. You may hit them, fair or foul, called strike or ball, or you will go out swinging or taking. The umpire will make each call.

"Good luck, boys!"

"Yes!" The players are eager to get their hits off Sammy.

Sammy and Jimmy did get a peek at the roster and standings, albeit brief as it is.

And the ump yells, "Batter up!" He points to Sammy.

Sammy winds up and throws a slider, swung on and missed. He pitches a strong Gyroball. The batter stood still, mesmerized for a called strike two. Jimmy calls for a Knuckle-Curve. This ball appeared to have come from the clouds and jumped past the batter for strike three.

"What is that he's throwing?"

"Dude, every pitch is a legal, Jimmy retorted, if not a rare pitch that Sammy has been throwing for years, well, minus his hospital stay." A lesson straight out of Coach Costello.

"Next Batter!"

Number two comes up to the plate to bat after practicing over half his training for Sammy's Fastball. The batter goes down swinging at three consistent Fastballs but to different locations.

The third batter singles into right field. One on, two out. The fourth batter fans on a Knuckle Ball, is tricked by a Cutter, then gets tricked and goes down by a pronator Breaking Ball.

"What the fuck was that?" The batter is visibly upset and confused.

"*Language!*" The umpire loudly snaps at the struck-out batter.

"OK boys. Next batter! Let's get to your warm up circles."

Jimmy signs once for three pitches; yes, the classics. Sammy whips a Fastball moving across the plate for strike one. He immediately goes into his wind up with the batter hardly prepared. It's another Fastball thrown pronator and a called strike. Sammy takes his time this pitch. Out from his mitt comes a moving, jumping Knuckle Ball. Strike three.

For the next sixty minutes, batters come up, and batters go down. The pitching display is nothing short of fully practiced and phenomenal. It's like none of the coaches have seen before; *ever*, not even in Major League bull pens. The players are confused. It is inspiring, extraordinarily so. Antithetical. Paradoxical. Hell. . . *Hostile!* And boy, are they happy!

The pronator is announced when a pronator is on the way but if you're sharp enough to catch a little spin, you might just pick up a hit. But it is much more than spin. It is ball movement. . .Backwards. Moose has a right-hander that can throw left side movers. And no matter the pronator or not, this boy has pin-point direction and target.

"Heck!" Coach Dunfeld exclaims. "Even his wind up is wizardly, like spookin' hound dog hoodoo out there.

"Wait till you guys see his Bean Ball!" Jimmy says with a grin. When a Sammy Fastball goes by a batter, it looks like the size of a small Aggie marble. A plate crowding batter is a prime target for a Bean Ball. Even though he's unlikely to be hit with the ball, he backs up after the threatening warning from the plate-owning pitcher.

"Oh Jesus H." Dunfeld mutters, as if starting a prayer.

Moose Coaching, and hitters get a good taste of Sammy Costello pitching along with the camaraderie of Jimmy Presta. For the umpire, not so much for the batter, Jimmy calls the pitch by name and if it will come pronator or not. The pronators appear as though they are coming from a hard lefty.

"Circle Change-up;

"Vulcan Change-up;

"Foshball;

"Curveball (Over-Arcing);

"Eephus Pitch;

"Spitball;

"Cutter;

"Knuckle Ball;

"Screwball;

"Gyroball;

"Split-Finger Fastball (Splitter);

"Curveball;

"Three-Seam Fastball;

"Two-Seam Fastball;

"Fastball;

"Knuckle-Curve."

Sammy delivers them all strong and on target.

Many of these pitches the coaches have never even heard of. They call a sit-in for the Coaching staff, Sammy, Jimmy and Art. First, the panel explains to the Coaches exactly what pronator muscle movement does. They tell the Coaches the type of adult, professional training that Sammy went through. . .Twice! And with him, Jimmy attends every practice religiously, as well.

The Coaches learn that Sammy, himself, on

his own, picked up pitching in between infield practices.

"You see, he was going to be a 2nd baseman. Sammy came to me with a compelling credo on the merits, as he put it, of pitching with control of the game, over an infield utility guy, reactionary playing a ball off the end of a bat. He prefers proactive to reactive ball-play. I'll let you guys read it."

"Sammy? Jimmy? Anything to add?"

Sammy says simply, "I want to win, batter by batter, and I know we all can do it."

"You should probably know that you just put down *the* best, *the* most elite hitting team in the division." Dunfeld says to Sammy and Jimmy.

"Well, Coaches," Art says. "I suggest firmly you study, even memorize Sammy's menu and understand every pitch. I would let Jimmy and

Sammy control the pitching game as much as possible, unless, of course, there's a call from the dugout. They will not disobey a call from the bench."

"I will never work any harder for any other pitcher." Jimmy says. "Sammy creates motivation."

Out of the blue, Dunfeld asks the catcher, "What's your hitting like, Jimmy?"

"Even though much of my time is taken up with Sammy," Jimmy says, "I am a power hitter. A natural, I guess. I led the league in home runs last year; just three above Jay Barfield. Nobody cares because I was on Kiwanis. Just call me Duke Simms!" McDowell cracks up: Duke was Sam McDowell's catcher.

"My guess is that you don't hit, huh, Sammy?

"Well, because I can so easily pick up

the spin of a pitch, I often get on with a single. Not always, but a fair percentage of the time, about .247 I guess."

"Well, Division A has the designated batter rule, but Division N does not. You'll be batting half the time."

25

Year one in the Babe Ruth League, Sammy wins all sixteen games by shut-out. He throws three no-hitters. His ratio of pitches to batters is 3.75. He's back. The bleachers are standing room only, and the fence is lined with spectators 'round the park for the final game of the season. With every pitch come cheers and applause. Sammy tips his cap every walk off the mound following every inning.

His hitters back him up scoring six runs; two 2-run dingers and two solo shots. . .one by Jimmy! Fives and knuckles all around, and by game's end, both teams line up for the congratulatory walk-by. Some players, voice low, simply say "good game." Others slap up or bust but almost all the losing team give it up for Sammy. . . "Awesome pitching, man". . ."Wow, how do you do it?", "Great pitching dude". And the like.

Art, playing the role of personal trainer and publicist turns down every interview requested. A play on words he often responds with are things like, "Too early to tell." After all, it was just one game. The bigger deal for Sammy is seeing Anita, Tristy, Mom, McDowell and Seaver in the stand's front row seats.

Wow, my whole family and Coaches are here!

Sammy did not disappoint.

"How does 'The Big Scoop' sound to everybody?"

"Let's go, Dad!" Sammy answers.

"What flavors this time?" Mom asks.

"I'm getting that new chocolate, coconut and pecan in a cup." Sammy certainly has his choice picked out. "It tastes like an Almond Joy gelato!"

"The fave every time," Tristy says like a deadbeat. "Mint Chocolate Chip, in a waffle cone."

"Vanilla cone dipped in chocolate for me!" Anita says. She sounds so happy lately. Sammy wonders why.

"What about you, Dad?"

"Chocolate in a cup," he says. "Large, that is.

"Mom?" Art asks.

"Vanilla cone."

"Oh, how exciting," Sammy says back with a laugh.

"OK. I am changing my mind! I am in the mood for a Cappuccino in a regular cone." Mom smiles at Sammy and her husband. "Medium."

She, Art, and Sammy laugh out loud.

"Going to remember all those in that elderly brain of yours?" Sammy chuckles with his Dad.

"Well, guess what titanium man, you are all going to order at the outside counter for yourselves. *Bam!*"

"Hey Sam," Dad calls. "Come into my office for a second? Have a seat."

"Yeah Dad?"

"We'll make this short, just a minute or two."

"OK."

"First, I want you to know how incredibly proud I am that you are my son." Art stops before his weepy eyes have a chance to leak out.

"Listen." Art fights back the tears. "I found out about the nasty things Grampy has been doing to you and Anita."

"He is fuckin' gross, Dad!"

He's never used any form of the 'F' word around the family and barely slips it out around his friends. His parents taught him well.

"Oh, I'm sorry, Dad."

"Don't be sorry, Sammy. Sometimes

situations come up where no other word will do. Situations like this."

"What's going to happen to him?"

"I'll take care of it from here. I just want you to know that he will never, ever be anywhere near us, any of us, ever again.

"That's it son. No more worries, OK?"

"Got it Dad! Whatever you did, thank you."

"Hey Sport?"

"Yeah?"

"Send Anita in here, would you, please?"

Moose plays Elks this weekend. They aren't much of a hitting team but are precise as a compass on the field. Dunfeld decides he isn't starting Sammy but he's not swapping him into 2nd base either. Sammy plays catch and practices some pitches with Presta, instead.

"Sammy," Jimmy calls out. "You've got a throw that is extremely effective but if we could get it to make its moves a little more dramatic, it would kill even worse than it does now."

"Yeah, so, what is it?"

"It's your Gyroball!"

"Yeah? It doesn't get hit much."

"Sammy, batters are already freaked out by it sailing in nice and easy, then boom, boom. It breaks high then low, just like that. If we could get those breaks just a little closer together, hitters have no chance. None. Any ideas?"

"I can change my grip slightly, and then throw it a little harder. If I throw it too hard, both breaks go away, and we have a fuckin' dinger, Jimmy."

"Well, it was just a thought. It's one hell of a pitch as is."

"Let's do something." Sammy says to Jimmy.

"What's that?"

"Let's work through our menu and take a good, long, hard look at all our work. Just to see if there is *any* room for advancement or improvement. This will include our Gyroball. What do you say?"

Jimmy says he thinks it's about time they did it. They sit at the picnic table behind the dugout and get to work.

"What are you guys doing?" Dunfeld asks.

Sammy says, "Something long in coming. Don't worry, it's all part of the job."

Dunfeld turns back to the game he is losing by one, and it's the last inning.

"Hey Presta!"

"Yeah Coach."

"Get in the on-deck circle. You're going up next."

Moose has one man on with two outs. Husky Jimmy Presta takes a few swings in the on-deck circle while Dunfeld explains the change to the plate umpire. Rosters are updated, And the ump is ready.

"Get in the box now, Presta."

"Give me a few swings ump. Jeeez!"

"Don't get wise kid."

"I'm about to get wise right *here*," he says as he grinds his cleats into his spot in the batter's box."

"Nope! **Ball**! *Low and in*," the umpire calls.

"Foul Ball. Out of Play!"

Here comes the curve. It's close but Jimmy takes it for a ball as it hits the dirt.

'Oh yeah. . .I know that windup. . .Give it to me rain man.'

And here comes the Palm Ball Change-up. Jimmy knows exactly where it's going. The lob is just below the letters, no movement and a little outside.

Jimmy swings, connects and that ball went off like a shotgun blast in the night. It coincidentally breaks right through the opposing Coach's car windshield. 'Well,' Jimmy's thinking trotting over 2nd Base, 'He ought to know better than to park right there in homer haven.'

26

Anita runs outside to get the mail every day. Her boyfriend, David was drafted and deployed to South Korea. They write to each other almost every single day. It's not as easy for him as it is for her to keep up the pace. He suggests that they write upon reply, which means she writes to him in a reply to his most recent letter, and he, in turn, does the same: He writes in a response to her most recent letter, it would better replicate a conversation-like writing exercise as opposed to stepping on each other's toes.

Art hears Anita whimpering in her room,

and lightly knocks on the door. "Anita? What's the matter sweetheart?"

"David doesn't love me anymore."

"Why do you think that?" Art asks. "Can I come in?"

"He's tired of writing to me, Daddy."

"Are you sure that's it, Anita?"

She hands her Dad the letter. He reads it through a couple times, then takes her hand and gives it a little squeeze.

"It makes good sense, Anita. Listen please: His days of his life in the service is full of orders, commands and deadlines. Besides that, think of how well we communicate face-to-face. We reply to one another. It's this method of correspondence that separates us, as a species from all others: meaningful interaction, calm and rational. It has nothing to do with a break-up, honey, nor is it a gauge of love."

"What if it is a grooming for break-up?"

"Anita, if a break-up comes along, there won't be any games. He, or you, will write it; simply, shootin' it straight. And I think each of you will do away with games, to briefly and cleanly cut away. I know you two are mature enough now to skip the bullshit and move on."

"So, this is just suggesting a new style of associating with each other?"

"Yes, Anita," Art answers. "I have to stand by that. A break-up is easy to pick up on. I do believe this is an attempt to take your connection to a higher level."

"Really think so?"

"Darling, he is thousands of miles away. Do you really think he feels compelled to stretch out a bad situation, or play with your heart? . . .I think not."

"Thanks, Dad." Anita says. "I feel so much better now."

Anita heeds the word of Dad but can't help but get a head start on her next letter to her boyfriend. She promises she will not mail it until she amends it with specific responses to what he should say to her in his next letter. She never realized how good and smart this relationship would feel. She feels a higher demeaner and more mature, delivered by way of Dad and her thoughts about what he said.

Much to everyone's happiness and good mood, all that squabbling that used to constantly occur between the two sisters has all but stopped completely. Sophia and Art know it has to do with the halt of Anita and Sammy's encounters with their now dead grandfather. They just *know* that has everything to do with it. The old, dry-as-the-desert sand of death is in an unmarked grave somewhere in the South End Cemetery.

Grammy Laura, Art's step mother dies shortly after the old man, but Art gives her a plot at the Costello family stone in Calvary Cemetery. Neither of them have a service of any kind. He was a monster and she was a ghost. And they are missed by nobody. Not one child of theirs show-up. And Art keeps it out of the papers and announces nothing. Not even the grands ask about them. Kids have a funny way of knowing who the creeps are.

27

Sammy is playing High School ball as well as Babe Ruth League and there is no indication of him ever slowing down. Art, McDowell and Seaver are fielding the scouts. They're everywhere. Phones don't stop ringing. Dinner invitations out keep pouring in. And no matter how polite they attempt to be, scouts will always be snakes in the grass.

"Well, son," Art says to Sammy. "You're nearing the end of High School, and I know we've had long talks about your next steps. You can pretty much have or take anything you want; you know that, right? So, tell me what you're thinking."

"Dad, I want to go to UNH. The University of New Hampshire has fantastic sport and athletic departments. Besides that, can you guess another reason I'd like to go there?"

"It's not hitting me over the head."

"My hero went there."

"Your hero. Let's count them all up by the hundreds!"

"Pudge, Dad! Pudge Fisk attended UNH! The incomparably *great* Carlton Fisk! The Commander!"

"Ah, yes. I should have known. He is one truly exceptional gentleman, and player."

"I'm going to take up where he left off."

"You know, Sammy, you've already got

massive heaps of Triple-A and Rookie scouts looking at you."

"I figured as much Dad. I see them climbing up your back, along with McDowell's and Seaver's.

"Yes, that's right. And it's never going to stop until you sign."

"I want to play for the BoSox."

"If you continue to play as you always do, you can play with anyone you want."

"Dad. . .Come on. . .Really?"

"I guess I always knew you'd want to go with your home town team. I'm certainly happy with your choices!"

"Have you read the Sports Section yet today?

"UNH scheduled the annual game against the Red Sox Double-A Rookie team!

"Dad, the skipper told us all about it the other day."

"And you didn't tell me?"

"O-M-G."

"Yeah. Geez, Sammy."

"They're not starting me."

"Any idea why not?"

"It sounds a little sketchy, but they said they wanted me for insurance. Not willing to share and show what they've got just yet."

"So, they don't want to overwork you but if your starter blows it, they're going to put you in for damage control to shut 'em down."

"That's essentially it, Dad, yeah. They said they may just put me in regardless, in the 6th or 7th inning."

"What a bunch of kooks."

"No matter what, I'll be ready, Dad."

"I've got no doubt about you, Sammy. But, I've seen enough of the rest of your teammates to know they could be easily dead to the Sox."

"Dad, if our hitters can hit, score a few runs, when I'm in there, the Sox don't have a chance."

"How's Jimmy doing with all this?"

"Nervous as a whore in church.

"All cut up like a boardinghouse pit.

"Dad. . .He's as nervous as a snake in a wagon rut. I told him to straighten out or I'm gonna slap his mother across the face!" Sammy is laughing so hard that it spreads to Art.

28

Art wants to be happy at his daughter Tristy's wedding. He put his best face forward. Doug insisted on ultra-formal wear; the long tails; the vest; the high stiff collar; corners down; the ribbon bow tie; the pocket square; men's lapel corsage; cuff links; black patent leather shoes. Doug wanted the works. No one else did but he got everything he wanted, except the top hats.

Tristy wants glamorous simplicity. Sounds cheap, doesn't it? But she chooses "The Ball Gown V-neck Court Train Satin Lace Wedding Dress, with the Ruffle." Not inexpensive. And yet she still manages to dress her half of the wedding party in the most hideously colored and some may say styled she could find: "Peach Vintage Empire Short Sleeve Zipper Chiffon Floor Length Bridesmaid Dresses." We've all seen worse but just a splash of orange tint anywhere in sight magically train the human eye to stare into it.

Because of the bride and groom's exquisite taste, or their need to show-off, Art makes a deal with Doug's father to go halves on the wedding expenses. Not just the clothes but the invitation packets, the announcements, the flowers, the cake, the entire reception. Art looks down at the line item expenses. The cost of an average American wedding is $16,000 to $20,000. This is too great a financial burden for either single family to bear. Today it is not unusual for the couple to pay for all wedding expenses or to have their parents and relatives equally contribute.

The Bride and her family pay for:

Wedding consultant;

Invitations and announcements;

Music for the wedding ceremony, including the organist or choir fee;

Flowers for church and reception;

Bouquets for the bride and bridesmaids;

Transportation of the bridal party to the church and reception;

Bride's gift to groom;

Bride's present to her bridesmaids;

Groom's wedding ring;

Church fee;

Lodging accommodations for out-of-town bridesmaids;

Various expenses related to the reception.

The Groom and his family pay for:

Bride's rings; engagement and wedding;

Boutonniere for the groom and ushers;

Groom's present to bride;

Groom's presents to ushers and best man;

Ties and gloves for the ushers;

Clergy member's cost;

Corsages for the immediate members of both families; also, the bride's going away corsage;

Bachelor dinner, usually given by best man or ushers;

Rehearsal dinner;

Accommodations for out-of-town ushers;

The honeymoon;

The Bridesmaids Pay for;

Dress and accessories;

Transportation to and from wedding, regardless of out-of-town expenses;

Gift to the wedding couple;

Contribution to a gift from all the bridesmaids to the bride.

The Ushers Pay for;

Rental or purchase of wedding attire;

Transportation to and from wedding, regardless of out-of-town expenses;

Gift to the wedding couple;

Contribution to a gift from all the ushers to the groom;

Bachelor dinner usually given by the best man.

The out-of-town guests pay for;

Transportation and lodging accommodations;

And a Gift for the wedding couple.

Art is not naïve in a single sense but is numb beyond wit at the articles considered, the costs of each, and wonders how, or if this is all necessary at all. So, the bride's and groom's fathers agree to pay half each for the entire extravaganza.

Tristy and Doug decide to settle in New Jersey, and make their honeymoon stop-over at The Poconos in Pennsylvania. Right in the middle of the frolicking and the Poconos romantic nonsense, Doug receives a telegram.

His father died suddenly of heart failure. Doug and Tristy quickly head down to Jersey to help Doug's mother with the arrangements. Doug is the named Executor in the will, anyway.

He is the only child of a couple that are successful family bankers. The businesses are left to Doug with a clause that also looks after his mother. Tristy feels sorrow but also salivates at the thought of how much money they stand to make. Wow. The president of a bank!

Every one of the Costellos dread the trip to New Jersey. Especially for an occasion like this. The dead man lay in the coffin looking like he came straight here from the wedding. Who knows? Maybe they are using the same tux! None of the Costello kids dare walk up to the casket. The girls are freaked out and Sammy is petrified to go any closer. The dead man's folded, crossed hands are abnormally long with long fingers. Sammy looks up at his Dad, and says, "Eww."

"Arachnodactyly, meaning 'spider fingers' or achromachia, Sammy," says Art. "It's a condition in which the fingers and toes are unusually long, boney and slender, in comparison to the palm of the hand and arch of the foot."

"How do you know about all this sh, er, stuff, Dad?"

"Your mother had an Uncle with the condition. I had to know, so I looked it up."

The man has a long horse-face that looks something like Fred Gwynne's "Herman Munster." Sophia and Art walk slowly to the kneeler, put their heads down, and say simply, "God bless this man."

SAMMY SCOUTS

29

The power the athletics department commands is incredible. They essentially get everything they ask for, big budget or small. Sammy and Jimmy are assigned dorm mates on the first floor of the Stoke Hall. It is the closest dwelling to the Baseball Field, Track, and the Athletics Department. They both reached the university by way of a Baseball Scholarship through the Portsmouth High School District.

Their Rookie stats recorded explain it all. Sammy has amassed a three-year stat sheet that reads like an MLB sheet: Better. But no one has ever seen inward college ball like it: No one has ever seen anything like it before. Games played equals Games won. Batters faced almost the same as Strike Outs. His ERA is *below one*. Base-on-Balls nears zero, infield hits occasionally but only every now and then.

Jimmy has a Batting Average of .686. He has a slugging percentage suggesting he's hitting 2B, 3B or homeruns 81 percent of the time. He has very few errors with a Fielding Percentage of .997. The Scouting and Rookie stats reports read like a fairy tale. But who are they, really, where are they? Where have they been?

Sammy and Jimmy can be seen on most days behind the draped bull pen warming up and practice pitching, during, before or after official practices. Scouts come with all their weapons of choice and ammo. Toys. Lazy.

Art insists on a Q & A Session with a

hand-selected small, limited group before opening the drapes tomorrow. He records the interview. The Scouts answer Art round-robin, a polling kind of way around the small group. The answers come in order, one-by-one, and some, quite verbose. They know what there is for them.

Art's first question is up. "Let's talk about Scouting Hitting. When you're watching a hitter for the first time, what are the things you like to see? What are you looking for?"

"The first thing is bat speed, whether it's wood or aluminum, just how fast can he swing the bat? That'd be the first thing and hopefully we get it with wood and can determine objectively what the bat speed is. And then his stance, his approach and does he have a feel to hit? Does he have a good knowledge of the strike zone?"

"All those things are kind of objective

there and you just kind of look at the hitter. "Sometimes those guys will just walk up to the plate and they'll walk up there with confidence and look like they can hit. So, you just kind of piece it all together?" Art asks.

"True. A lot of what I'm looking for goes beyond what they're doing at the plate. You like to see the athleticism and the sort of body that is going to continue to get better. Guys that physically are what they are when they're sixteen years old, it's difficult to project that guy out significantly."

"It's nice when a guy passes the eye test right when he steps off the bus, right?" Art laughs.

"Or, when I walk up to the field and I don't need to get a program to figure out which kid he is. At the plate, generally I'm looking at the mechanics of their swing and the bat speed that they have. You try to get into pitch recognition and plate discipline and things like that but that really turns into one of the most difficult things for high school hitters because they're not seeing quality breaking balls and they're generally not seeing velocity.

"The single biggest thing for me, and I write it down all the time, is 'handsy' looseness to the swing. In other words, just that little whip in the bat with the hands instead of the strength. And I know there are different types of guys with the strength swings, but those guys are different types of birds. We don't see those guys very often. And I think those guys still have the 'handsy' looseness, it just comes through as strength because of their bodies. But that 'handsy' looseness, I've never seen a guy that didn't have that pan out and become big time major league hitters. It's just that point in the swing where the top hand starts to move the bat. When the top hand starts to bring the bat head through the zone, those hands right there. How fast can they whip that bat? When a pitch is on the way, only those special guys really have that bit of whip there to really get that bat head moving and get it in the right spot to make sure you square up the ball."

"I would think that it depends on when you're watching him," Art joins-in. "Right? So, if it's pregame and we're just watching batting practice, pregame is nice, you can learn some things about it but it's not everything. I don't want to get too excited and I don't want to get too down, either. In batting practice I'm looking for bat speed; I'm looking at the bat path; I'm looking at his balance, and I'm looking at how his hands work. Do they work independently, or does he kind of swing with his shoulders? I really like guys that have good hands.

"I'm looking for a short path that has some pop. It also depends on the position. If I know the guy plays a corner, I'm looking bat and power. I want to see some thump and if you're not thumping it, you better steal a ton of bases.

"Once the game starts, I'm looking for a guy that can hit deep in the count, that can hit in tough situations and that flat out hits the ball hard often. If you can't make contact, what good are you? That's the biggest thing with hitters. Hitters hit. They hit the ball hard." Art waits for a response.

"Right, so we watch how the ball comes off the bat. How much raw power does the kid generate? Does he have some lift to his swing, does he have some loft? If he has some loft to his swing, that tells you with some raw power, he's going to hit some homers. If he doesn't generate any loft, he's going to be a doubles and singles kind of guy. I watch for the way he holds the bat. If he holds the bat back in his palms, then it's going to be a little tougher to hit. It's going to create some tension in his swing and not so much 'wristy' action. It's kind of a negative if they hold the bat farther back in their palms."

"Some scouts like it more than others but what are your thoughts on watching players take batting practice?" Art asks.

"I like batting practice because I think your plate swing is basically the same as it is in batting practice. Your ability to adjust obviously comes into play when it's game speed but you can get a good look at a player's pure mechanics in practice. But I think a lot of guys put too much into it.

You walk out of there and the kid has missed two or three Curveballs by a foot and gets jammed with an 87 MPH Fastball because he doesn't have enough bat speed and a guy's walking out of there still talking about the batting practice and I'm like, 'Dude, did you see the three freaking at-bats?' It's still about the game."

"You see how a player approaches batting practice. Does he use the whole field to hit? Usually in a batting practice round, the batter will try and go the other way for the first round and then the second round, he'll hit the ball where it's pitched and then maybe the third round he'll show his power to wherever that is, right field or left field. And then the path of the bat. Does he hit a lot of fly balls? Does he hit a lot of ground balls? Is he a line-drive hitter? Does he square it up hard?"

"Obviously batting practice pitchers don't throw very hard and you like to see a guy square a ball up consistently pretty hard in batting practice. A red flag would be a lot of swing and misses in BP or a couple swing and misses and fouling off the ball in the cage. That's a good indicator of hand-eye coordination. So, definitely how he approaches batting practice and how hard does he square it up in batting practice."

"I think it's huge," Art adds. "For me, it's huge, because in the ballgames, I would say 75 percent of the high school kids we go watch are not getting pitched to. So, to be able to go see BP ahead of time and multiple times, that's huge for me. You can see how the swing works and what type of raw power he has. A lot of times, you like to go when they don't know you're there watching. In my area, kids take BP before the game on the field and I know a lot of places in the country, that doesn't happen.

"How many times do you like to see a hitter before you're comfortable putting a grade on his tools?"

"For me, Art, of course over a couple of years with a college guy and you hope to see him a couple of times per year. The most difficult thing for me is when I go to see guys out of my area and I walk in on those really good players, guys that I know are good, and they don't have a good day or something and you have to ask yourself, 'OK, what did I see in BP? What did I see in his swings in the game, even though he didn't hit anything?' And then throw a grade on him, that's tough to do at this point. I guess the answer is at least a half a dozen times before I feel comfortable. As many as possible, basically."

"Well, I like to see one batting practice to see his raw power, see basically how far he can hit it. One batting practice I'm good with but obviously, the more times you can see a hitter, the better. It depends on the game. If you go to a game and the guy gets pitched to and he squares a ball up and pretty much shows you what you think he's got, one game would be sufficient to write him up. But sometimes you might go to the game and he gets walked twice, or maybe he has a poor at-bat on the breaking ball, he waves at the breaking ball and he only gets three at-bats. Maybe it's a left-handed hitter facing a left-handed pitcher and the guy struggles off the left-handed pitchers, so you think he might be a platoon guy and you have to come back and see him against a right-handed pitcher."

"Just once," Art says. "I mean, you either get that fuzzy feeling, or you don't. If you get that fuzzy feeling, then it's on to the games to see how he takes pitches, how quiet he is at the plate. That's huge for me. You want to make sure his hands don't go forward, or he doesn't lunge when he's taking pitches. If he's quiet taking pitches, then you know he's going to be a good professional hitter. If you get that fuzzy feeling one time around, you've got to write him up. Pretty much, you should, to start the process of getting your supervisors in to see him. The longer you wait, the longer it takes your supervisor to get in there, because everybody else in the nation wants their guys looked at too. It's a long process to be able to get a kid seen by the people who make decisions."

"Well, I generally like to see guys with fairly calm approaches at the plate. An excessive movement, be it a high leg kick or a hitch with their hands or just anything that can alter the timing and execution of the swing, I don't like. That's not to say there aren't guys that do those kinds of things and are extremely successful doing it, like ol' Yaz did but I feel like those guys are the exception and the fact is that when you slow them all down, when their foot's down and their hands are ready to go, they're just about all in the exact same position.

"It doesn't matter if it's Manny Ramirez with the high leg kick or Gary Sheffield with the bat waggling. You slow down the video and they're in the same spot when they're ready to hit. Getting into that position consistently is a lot harder if you're moving around a bunch. Another thing I really don't like to see is head movement in a swing. You can't hit if you can't see it. So, any sort of thing where a player moves his head during a swing, it's difficult for that player to consistently center the ball against better competition."

"OK, guys," Art says. "Let's talk Scouting Pitching.

"When you're watching a pitcher for the first time, what are you looking for?"

"First, it's his arm slot. Is he sidearm or three-quarters, high three-quarter or overhand? And then his arm swing in the back. Is it clean in the back? Or is it short and compact? Is it rigid? And then arm speed coming through. Does he have a live arm? That's really the first thing because the guy that has a slow arm, obviously, isn't going to throw very hard. And then his size. Traditionally, you want a guy 6-foot-1 or above, because that's going to give him leverage and create plane on the Fastball to home plate. The ability to spin the breaking ball, too, especially a high school kid. He's got to be able to spin either the Curveball or the Slider.

"A lot of times there's been guys with good arms that don't have a feel to spin it but then they get in the minor leagues and not only do they have to have success with getting hitters out when they're learning a breaking ball, it's tough for them. It's something that I'd really like to see a young high school pitcher have, is the ability to spin the breaking ball with a good tight spin and have some feel for it. A college guy, obviously, better have a feel of some type of breaking ball to have any type of success at the college level and then, of course, at the pro level, too."

"It's always been about stuff, just pure stuff. Fastball, Curveball, Change-up. You know, what do those things do now and what are they going to do in the future? The projection, for me, is not so much the body. We all like the big, projectable body and windup, and you know what that looks like.

But it's not so much that than it is the arm speed. If you want to throw 90 MPH, you must make your arm go 90 MPH. It's simple but that's the biggest thing I look at if I think they're going to project and get those pitches to get better.

"The second thing is, and I'll go to my grave with this one. I follow all the guys I've scouted with this, and that's if they are strike throwers in high school, I don't care if they're throwing 85 MPH but if they're strike throwers in high school, they're going to continue to be strike throwers. But if they're not, they are not going to become strike throwers.

"I don't care if Houdini works with them or the other best pitching Coach in the world, whoever that might be. If you don't throw strikes at a young age, you're not going to learn how to throw them. To me, that's the biggest thing. I've drafted some big arms and they've made it to the big leagues as relievers or whatever but they're always going to give their managers headaches because they'll be like, 'Can he throw a strike?'"

"You hate to say it but guys, listen to this, please. Velocity is kind of the first thing that jumps out at you. There are plenty of kids out here that can pitch but are throwing 80 and that just isn't going to work. I like to see athleticism in the delivery, a repeatable delivery and a low-stress delivery, something where they're not significantly fighting their body to throw quality strikes."

"I don't like to see a lot of side-to-side movement—pitchers that either throw across their body or stride open and open their front side early. Generally, that creates a lot more stress in the delivery and it's going to hinder their command and their stuff. The goal this guy has is getting the ball on a straight line to the plate. If they have that side-to-side movement, they create momentum with their body toward either first base or third base. They must then fight back to get to the plate and throw strikes. So, as much as guys can minimize that, is certainly a good thing. And you want to see a delivery that works together, the bottom half and the upper half, so a guy's not just throwing all arm. The more athletic the guy is, the more apt he's probably going to be to make these sorts of adjustments.

"If you have a guy who isn't particularly athletic and has a high-maintenance delivery, it's going to become difficult for that guy, as he becomes physically mature, to straighten out his delivery. It's nice when you go in to see a pitcher and then the next day he's playing Shortstop or Center Field or catching and hitting. Those are the type of athletes that you're looking for.

"I feel that if a kid is athletic and shows some aptitude on the mound, then a lot of those delivery flaws are fixable. I tend to think arm action is arm action. The first time you pick up a ball and throw it is generally how you throw and trying to change someone's arm action isn't a particularly successful practice. Most of the guys get hurt or they lose their stuff. It's kind of a fine line where some people have to make a decision: Are they going to continue pitching in a way that is likely to get them hurt but maintain their stuff, or are they going to take a risk and see if they can maintain their stuff while changing their arm action significantly?"

"What about arm action," Art asks. "I look

at how clean and easy it is or appears. But it depends, you know, because a lot of relievers in the big leagues throw with some sure-fire effort. I think it's hard to find starters. Number one, I'm looking for athleticism or a guy that can repeat his delivery consistently. If he can repeat it, there's a good chance he can repeat it with a Fastball, which means he's going to be able to locate his Fastball. And, if he's a dude-real, he should be able to locate his secondary pitches also. Starters, for me, should have at least three average pitches or better with, plus control. If it's a lefthander, I'll give him a little bit of the benefit of the doubt on the Fastball velocity if he can paint and mix."

"The biggest thing though, for me, if you're a starter, especially if you have average stuff, you better be able to command it. You better be able to have some Fastball sink or exceptional movement. Because if it's just straight or it's just fringy movement, you don't have a chance, dude, you're going to get hammered and dinged all day long. The more movement, the better. That's why everyone wants a Halladay, because the movement is ridiculous."

"OK, then the delivery: how his arm action is in the back and how the ball comes out of his hand. A lot of times we're always worried about, if he doesn't have the prettiest arm action, is that an injury waiting to happen down the road? If it's a clean arm action and the ball comes out good, but the velocity might not be there, well you can project that when he gets bigger and stronger. The velo's going to be there because he has good arm action, he's clean.

"I look where his front foot lands, too. If his front foot lands open, if he's a right-handed pitcher and his left toe is pointing to the first base dugout, that's not good. That's muscle memory and it's hard to get a kid out of that. You don't want to land with an open heel because you're losing velo and you're losing your lower half there. I'm not saying it can't be corrected but pitching coaches I've talked to say it's hard to get a kid out of it. Unless the kid's blowing 92-94 MPH already, well then you can live with it. But if he's 88-90, well, he's generic then."

"What do you like to see and what don't you want to see when it comes to a pitcher's mechanics?" Art asks the group.

"For me, as a scout, if I don't see any major red flag areas, I'm okay with the delivery and I know our guys are good enough that they'll tweak him to where he can do things a little bit better, so I don't concern myself with that too much. I'm kind of a big mouth but I go down the side like everybody else does with a right-handed pitcher, you know, down the third base line. And when I'm walking down, I always go, 'I'm just walking down here to BS, fellas. I'm not quite sure what to look at down here.'

"Some scouts will watch a pitcher's mechanics and they'll go, 'See, he got over his front leg!' And I'm just like, 'Let me tell you something. I don't care if he got over his front leg or not, that Curveball just went like this and their best hitter just swung and missed at it.' You can go over your front knee all you want but if you don't have any stuff to get him out, you're not going to be any good."

"Right! Usually the guys that repeat their delivery better are the guys that are more athletic. For example, men with effortless movement are ultra-athletic. If you've ever seen a good pitcher golf, he's usually an impressive golfer. When we're talking arm action, ideally you want a cleaner circle. You don't want a stab or a jab, where they're basically stabbing their arm back and it doesn't come out of the glove as a clean circle, because that action, as your body moves forward, is very hard to repeat.

"Everyone's got a little flaw here and there but the reason we want those arm actions to be like a clean full circle, or a medium circle, or even like a Bartolo Colon who had a short circle in his prime, it's because circles are like a timing mechanism and they end up being on time more often than a guy that stabs or stops his arm. You've still got your Rick Sutcliffes, who plunge their arm down and come back up There are some exceptions to the rule but in most cases, that's kind of the ideal arm action we're looking for and that helps with repeating your delivery and delivering the baseball.

"So, we can say, 'Hey, this is what we want.' But do you know what the reality is? So, there's an ideal model I think we're all looking for but we're also not going to ignore the guy that has a great feel for repeating his delivery and timing. So, while that windup is impeccable, consistent along with multi-locations are a topper."

"More red flags?" Art asks his panel of scouts.

"Mechanically, a real short arm action in the back. Maybe a low-slotted elbow, when the elbow's lower than the shoulder and just pushing the ball toward the plate, that would tend to create problems over the long haul. And this happens with most players, most of them stand straight up and down, nowadays.

"They don't get good extension out front and they don't finish the pitch. And I'm talking about finishing the pitch with the hand outside of the knee on the land leg there. They all stand straight up and down, and I believe that they do that because it's physically easier to finish the pitch standing straight up and down. But with that, they're not going to get extension and the ball is going to have the tendency to be up in the strike zone more, and with less velo. Extension is the one thing that I don't see a lot of pitchers get out there in the amateur world. And when you do see it, he definitely stands apart."

Art asks, "What kinds of things do you look for that make you think someone will add velocity down the line?"

"Good question, Art. First and foremost, if he's a max effort guy and he's already maxing out, he's probably going to go backward. It's kind of like a four-cylinder engine on a vehicle—the harder that it's got to work to go uphill, eventually the guy that's a V-8 can get up the hill a little easier. Loose, as in it comes out with a little less effort. It looks like he's playing catch, right? The reason we want those guys is because if they work at a lower effort and they can maintain velocity, they're going to probably be able to go a little harder maybe when they need to or probably be able to maintain that 92-95 MPH Sinkerball through nine innings without a problem."

"Guys. . .Come on. First, it's the eye test. We're looking for tall, lean, and I'm not going to say skinny kids but non-mature kids that three or four years down the road, they're going to get in the weight room to where you can project that they are going to throw harder. If you go out there and you already see a mature kid that's 87-90, well I don't know how much you can project any more in that. But, if you get the skinnier kid or the leaner kid with good arm action that's already sitting 89-91, you're going to believe he's going to eventually add more velo to his Fastball."

"As scouts, we're hoping to project on a kid. I don't like going to the ballpark and the 18-year-old senior is already a man and there's no projection there, it is what it is. I think, as a scout, the worst thing a kid can have as a high school senior or even a high school junior is a beard. That's not good. You walk into a ballpark and you've never seen the kid yet, but you walk in and he's got a fully-grown beard. That tells me he's mature and there's not projection there. It's all about perception. Perception is 90 percent of it. Whether it's right or wrong, if I walk into a ballpark and I see a kid with a beard and he's just OK, well I can't project anymore. The kid's fully matured. That's one thing for me, I like baby-faced guys."

They all laugh.

"OK, we'll spend a little time on Scouting Defense, but I'd like to focus on the Catcher, primarily.

"When you're watching a player defensively, what are you looking for, and what are some of the specific requirements for different positions?"

"You want a guy with a good first step toward the ball. They should be light on their feet and it doesn't look like they're wearing concrete shoes. Because you've got to go laterally to put yourself in position to field a ground ball or one in the dirt. Some kids have got it and some kids don't. Usually the Shortstops got it, most of the time. If they're a high school Shortstop that can't run and doesn't have footwork, well, guess what? They're moving to third base or maybe become an offensive second baseman."

"Generally, it all kind of works from the ground up. Agile, athletic guys that are light on their feet. That's the first part. And then, their hands are second. That really plays at just about any defensive position. It's a little less important in the outfield but particularly with catchers and middle infielders, you want good hands and good feet. For arms, it's disappointing that we're not seeing the same quality of arms that we used to overall, not just in amateur scouting but in pro ball.

"People have gotten away from a lot of things that help allow you to develop arm strength. Now, 12-year-olds have structured pitching programs, whereas in the past, they pitched, they played Shortstop, they long tossed and just threw a ball more consistently. Every time you see a kid on a baseball field now, he has a uniform on, and it used to be that you could see kids in shorts and a T-shirt and four guys on each side, improvising some way to play a game. Now you have two games a week and a practice and that's all the time they spend on that. I think arm strength is the one tool that is most dependent on just doing it, just repeating the activity."

"You can do whatever weight training you want to do and some of that can help and some of it can hurt but the only way to get better at throwing a baseball is by doing it. It's such a specialized athletic motion, so that's about it. By the time guys are on our radar for the draft, I feel with most of them, what you see is what you get, for their arms."

"Outfield-wise, oh boy. . . it's a real crapshoot. To see an outfielder, do just a few things, shoot, you might have to watch nine games."

"You want to get there early and watch him

take groundballs and infield practice. While they're taking batting practice, see how he shags them off the bat, if he does shag them off the bat. Maybe he's the type of guy that doesn't do that. That tells you a little bit about the guy, too.

"But *maybe* he's power shagging out there, taking all kinds of balls off the bat in the infield or outfield. And then, of course during the infield practice, you really bear down on him to look at his instincts and his actions and his range and his arm strength to get a feel for the glove."

"BP, Batting Practice, is huge to watch them take grounders before the game. We don't get a lot of time to get multiple looks early, so what we see during in and out, is huge. We've got to see the actions and see the foot work. If the feet work and he has good actions, well there's something there to work with. Obviously arm strength is a part of it too. *What I don't like as a scout is when the infielders just half-ass the ball over to first and don't show any arm strength. We've got to see the arm strength. When we don't see it, we have to project it.*"

"The first thing is arm strength. If they don't have arm strength very much, for me, you can't do much with them. Hopefully it's a 45 arm if they can block and have good fundamentals behind the plate. They receive the ball well and have soft hands. You look for footwork too. If their feet work on the transition, are they light on their feet to explode through second base, or do they just stand up and not use their feet to throw? Basically, if you don't have arm strength, you better do all the other stuff average to above to offset it. If you have arm strength, the other stuff can be taught. You have to believe the other stuff can be taught."

"An ability to be able to throw guys out is right up there with his receiving ability to be able to catch pitches. You must be athletic back there because you do have to move quick and have lateral range. Good size is important because that's a wear-and-tear position over the long haul. The ability to frame and give the umpire a good look on borderline pitches.

"Definitely you don't want to scout a Catcher that's going to drop a lot of balls during a game. That's going to tell you a lot about his hands. Maybe he doesn't have the best hands, and the guy he's catching probably has below average stuff, compared to the pro level. So, you want to see a guy catch 99 percent of his pitches that's being thrown to him and not maybe drop but one, or none."

"And we all love our big, hitting Catchers, right?"

"Damn straight, Art!"

"I'd really like to see the guy probably three or four games with a couple of batting practice sessions in there. You try and match those high school hitters up against someone that's at least going to pitch to them and potentially challenge them and see them against some sort of level of competition that isn't just someone throwing 75 MPH. A lot of the process in getting comfortable with these players is seeing them on the showcase circuit the summer before, so you have that follow number on the guy and you've had the opportunity to see them against some competition and then you go back in the spring and figure out if you got the guy right or you need to make an adjustment on him.

"With the hitters, I'd like to get as many at-bats as possible. It's certainly easier with the college guys because the matchups are significantly easier. The high school guys, you have to figure out which ones you like and get in and see them."

"What are you looking for mechanically in a hitter's swing? What sorts of things are red flags for you?"

"A lot of guys talk about a hitch not being correctable but if a hitch is a timing mechanism, I think it's OK. If a hitch occurs during the swing and causes the bat to be late, then I do think you have a problem on that because that involves their hand-eye coordination when the ball is released and when they recognize it and so forth. So, a hitch bothers me if it's part of their swing and not a timing mechanism but that hitch, it's a timing mechanism and that bat's in the right spot when it needs to be. The arm bar doesn't really bother me because I think you can help that if you need to help it but there's a lot of major league batters that arm bar but then get that bat going out there good enough. I think you can learn to help a guy develop not to do that. I don't know if there's any one thing that I would say 'Wow, that one can't be fixed.' Other than just a slow bat. Slow bat's a slow bat. If you don't have bat speed, I don't think you're going to develop it."

"Maybe a kid, no matter what his stance is, whether it's square or it's open, and he steps in the bucket, maybe he's showing you that he has a little fear of the ball and that kind of raises the yellow flag. Swinging at the breaking ball out of the strike zone consistently, that may show you that he can't identify the pitch or can't lay off the pitch and that's tough to correct, too." -[1]-

"Oh my God, those scouts can chatter! I'm tired just having contributed and facilitated!"

30

This is by far the most bizarre and secretive demonstration any of the scouts have attended, or in this case, been invited to. The diamond is walled-off with tarp in the school colors sky-blue and white. There are a few mitt-men working on their playing arms in the outfield.

Sammy and Jimmy prep their workstations and then both sit in the shade of the dugout. Art stands in the on-deck circle and invites the selected scouts to step up to hear him, and briefly introduces his son and Jimmy to the men.

He explains to them that this will have been only the second of just two demos that anyone, anywhere will have had the opportunity to experience. He encourages the use of their toys, but suggests strongly they suit up in either catcher gear or home plate umpire gear for close-up observation.

"That way," Art suggests. "You will see the full effect of every pitch. What you are about to witness is a pitch-through of a menu of Major League Baseball throws. Sammy compiled the menu before Little League. He mastered the entire menu and quickly became the star of the show."

He tells them about the hit he took, putting him in the coma. And is happy announcing the 100% recovery. Of course, there is a lot of therapy and relearning his pitch menu. He praises Jimmy for his part in joining, like a brother, Sammy to work it all through. They worked several hours six days a week with each.

"Their second Little League year for them was underplayed but they were known as "The Saviors." Once High School ball and Babe Ruth League began, word started getting out. We all wanted to keep the phenoms behind the curtain. But the press bled out leak after leak highlighting Sammy's gifts, and Jimmy's support, and that is of the team, as well, not just Sammy. Jimmy's Field PCT is .997 and his Batting AVG is .608 and has a Homerun tally likely never to be topped. But most of all, he is half of Sammy's talent out there. They know exactly what they're doing out there, and what each other is thinking. That's how tight they are.

"So, gentlemen, station yourselves where you wish. Jimmy will sign Sammy but for your benefit will give an audible of Pitch and whether it is a pronator throw. There is one more thing you should be prepared to take-in today. Nearly every pitch that breaks in the slightest may be thrown pronator, or not. Jimmy will call when a pronator pitch is coming in."

". . .pronator?"

". . .pronator?"

Sammy toes the rubber and tosses a few warm-up throws. He flips his glove and Jimmy says, "We're set when you guys are."

"Top of the Menu, down. Go ahead, guys!"

"Fastball."

"103 miles per Hour!" A scout yells.

"Curveball."

"Curveball Pronator."

"Holy-shit! Did you guys see that? He just threw a lefty curve with his right hand!"

"Calm down, man."

"Gyroball."

"Did that thing rise or fall?"

"Both, sir."

"Eephus Pitch: The ultimate down pitch."

"Holy Cow!"

"Slurve: Combo Curveball and Slider."

"Pronator."

"Cutter."

"Pronator."

"I cannot *believe* what I am seeing here!"

"Cutter."

"Sharpest Cutter I've ever seen!"

"Pronator!"

"Knuckle Ball."

"Knuckle-Curve."

"Wait. No one throws those for real. They just say they do, for effect."

"Pronator."

"In all sincerity," Jimmy says "Would you like a closer look? Come on into the batter's box."

Sammy finishes up with his entire series of Fastballs and Curveballs, Pronators included. He throws his Foshball, among a whole series of wicked mean Change-ups.

Jimmy calls, "Finale!"

Then, *"Screwball!"*

"Pronator!"

Art tells all the gentlemen that he hopes they honor the vow to secrecy in what they just saw out there. Only four others have witnessed the incredible power, control and the result of a lifetime of training; Sam McDowell, Tom Seaver, Art, Coach Marusso and Coach Dunfeld.

"Just stating a simple fact, we chose you out of a pool of well over a hundred. We've always shrouded ourselves in modesty, because Sammy and Jimmy have gaming merit, integrity and are men's men."

"Art! Art!" A scout cries out. "Will Sammy finish school here at UNH, no matter?"

"No matter what, what? Yes, indeed he will. He has a deal-breaker GPA that can keep in school ball, or out."

"So, Art," One scout confirms. "You are giving our group of scouts, that's us, exclusivity?"

"Besides Mr. McDowell and Mr. Seaver, yes. So, respect it. You are scouts; not press journalists, mugs as they are."

"Here, here!" Everyone laughs.

Art suggests they meet right back here after lunch. They'll eat at a special little place Art enjoys every time he eats there. It's one of those holes in the wall with exquisite food and service places. The two boys will eat at the cafeteria.

"I'm sure you'll like it. I ask we stay out of all soliciting at the table. Base questions are okay but nothing more business oriented."

"Art, do Sammy and Jimmy come as a package deal?"

"Without a doubt, yes, they do. You won't find another more dedicated pair of team mates. Plus, they've grown and trained together their entire lives. What's more is that they are true best friends. They are also devoted to the game and their respective jobs in every game."

"Do they realize the spectacle going on all around them, secrecy or not?"

"Yes, of course they do. . .Ever since Little League but they were raised humble, thankful, grateful and to *practice, practice, practice!* Ah! Yes, the food is here, so, let's back-off now."

31

Anita's latest boyfriend is a Greek guy in the Marines. His name is so long that no one can pronounce it but, it has a couple occurrences of a "bo" syllable in it, so everyone just calls him "Bo." While awaiting discharge, he is assigned an assistant to the Warden of the prison at the Portsmouth Naval Shipyard. Art likes him. He wears several medals for his accomplished deployment to Vietnam, though most of his deployment he spent in De Nang ingesting magic potions and screwing as many of the youngest and tiniest girls wherever he can find them. And here, Art makes sure Bo has a job uninterrupted when he is finally Honorably Discharged.

The couple and the family enjoy a more casual wedding than Tristy. And just after moving into a nice second floor apartment in Portsmouth's South End, Anita announces that she is pregnant. Art offers to pay their rent for a year to help them out. She gives birth to a stunning baby daughter in early February, just after her own birthday in January, which forgoing stretches the Christmas Season out even longer.

Since both young parents work, Grammy Sophia babysits her granddaughter every day. They form a bond that most children do not even get to forge with their own parents, let alone grandparents. The infant is adorable, and when Sammy is home from campus, he sees a lot of the kid around the house.

Sammy has two days' rest before practice begins for the BoSox Rookies at UNH game. Jimmy and Sammy play catch in the morning and take advantage of coach's orders and rest the hot day long afterward. They suicide-bodysurf across the street from the small pub "Rye on the Rocks" at the beach end of Washington Road.

The water is never more than the mid-fifties, and the currents are athletically challenging. The rocky coast of New England is no less present here than anywhere else along Massachusetts, New Hampshire and Maine coasts. Hence, the 'Suicide' sobriquet.

The two nights prior to the big game, the boys review the BoSox Rookie roster to identify the hitters and types of hitters they'll go up against, in case they are put into the game. Art acquires, as he so often does, the UNH lineup stapled to the roster.

"Our lineup is full of big hitters, top to bottom. Big Bad John is our designated batter." Art tells them what they really want to know.

"Boys, you will not be starting."

"Why not, Dad?"

"The Coach is not yet confident in his relief pitcher program. He has three low key starters besides you two big-gamers. He knows *your* starting debut will be a day of history in the making."

"Hmmm, shit," Sammy sighs. "I get it, okay." He says frustratingly so.

"Language Sam. My prediction is that he's going to get into trouble, probably early, and when he does, enter, Sammy Costello and Jimmy Presta.

"Not to make light of the potential situation, I suggest you two work through your relief sequences, along with all your batter-open pitches. All week. Seriously. Got it?"

"Got it, Mr. Costello!" Jimmy says, then, "Whew!"

Anita comes barreling up the driveway. Sophia notices her driving is erratic and too fast, and she can be heard crying from all the way out by the pool. Anita sits slouched forward with her head resting in her hands, on the steering wheel. Sophia sees she is crying so hard that she is convulsing and shuddering.

Sophia picks-up the baby and rushes over to Anita's car. She dares not try to make her daughter talk now, so she stands next to the car, just behind Anita's left shoulder, but she must ask.

"Anita, sweetie, what's the matter?"

It seems like too long a time before Anita can catch her breath enough to speak a word. Sophia takes the small child to the playpen set up in the living room for the time being, as the little one begins to cry, too.

"Anita, dear," Sophia says. "Come with me to the porch where we can relax. Come on sweetie. You can tell me all about it."

"Mommy," Anita is struggling to get the words out. "My Bo doesn't love me anymore."

"What? How do you know that? What happened?"

"Bo doesn't love me anymore. I lost my Bo." Anita bursts into more tears. Her mother holds her hand nice and tight. They sway together on the bamboo rocking love seat for what seems like forever, but it's twenty minutes and by now, Anita is calmed enough to speak.

Art drives slowly up the hill and up to the right-side garage door. He gives the horn two quick toots and jumps out of the car. He shuts the door behind him and walks through the breezeway into the breakfast nook, and on through the kitchen.

He hears Sophia and Anita talking, and by the resonation of things, it doesn't sound good. The baby is quiet and about to fall asleep in her playpen. He tip-toes by on his way to the front door. It leads into the glass porch where the voices are coming from.

He walks around in front of his two girls and sits next to Anita. He snugs-in as close as he can. He says nothing but sways with them. Anita's tears well up again when Daddy comes in. He gives her all the time she needs.

Sophia mouths the words over Anita's bowed head for Art.

"Bo left Anita."

It takes every heartbeat of energy for Art to hold it in. He's borderline shocked. He manages to address his young daughter.

"Darling Anita, please try to gain enough composure to tell me what is happening. Please, sweetheart."

After a moment, she begins speaking with her father.

"Daddy, I got home just a little earlier than usual. I'm glad because I get to see him before he leaves for work. He ignores me until I reach the kitchen but then lifts his head and screams at me. He says, *"Fuck! Why the fuck are you home so early?"*

"He is writing a note but when he sees me, he crumbles it up and flings it to the floor.

He screams at me again, *'I am leaving you! I do not love you and I am leaving!'*

"But, why? What did I do? What is wrong?" I ask him.

"He says, 'when you got pregnant, you got ugly! I couldn't stand the sight of you!'

"Bo that happens to a lot of girls but then things turn back. I told him. I'll be the girl you love again soon. I know I will."

He then says to her, in a more impassive voice, "Look, Anita, over the course of eight and a half ugly months here, I fell in love with somebody else."

"But Bo, we can fix things." Anita says. "We have a beautiful baby daughter together. Please."

"There will be no 'fixing' Anita. Divorce papers are drawn. You'll have been served them by the weekend."

And to her concerned parents, she says in a whimper, "That's the last thing I heard as he trampled downstairs and slammed the front door. He must have already packed a bag or something for himself."

Art takes two days away from his downtown office and tends to a few things at home, from his office there. He makes call after call to every law official agency in the region. He calls bureau chiefs everywhere, the Chambers of Commerce and Business Owners, most of whom he is on a first name basis with.

Finally, he calls out to his lawyer, who is also the county judge, to help handle the Divorce through court, as Art vows to make this the most expensive Divorce case Bo will have ever seen and certainly experience. Art has seen it written before:

"You best know who you be fucking with, boy."

"Yes, Judge," Art says. "I know there'll be hefty alimony and high standard child support. I want him to have to purchase a home for her, or at the very least provide rent at an upper-middle-class level. I also want her in a new, dependable, reliable automobile. And let's not forget the verbal assault and abuse. I want 'abandonment' written-in to the charges. And they have a new-born baby girl, for Christ's sake!"

"We can do this, Art."

"Thanks very much Tom your Honor Flynn."

His next series of calls go out to every business registered with the Chambers of Commerce. His message for each is nearly the same.

"This man is not to be trusted, and therefore not to be hired. He is a Greek activist with a sketchy past. He'll stay where he is or go nowhere. Handle it, gentlemen, so I do not have to step-in, because, if pushed, you know I will."

To the layers of law enforcement, Art warns of, "an unstable man, unpredictable, abusive, unsafe and perilous driver, to the level of chronic. He carries weapons with him always. He is a Greek activist with a checkered past. This man is not fit to carry."

Bo's place of business is told to keep him there but to *not* write any letters of reference but if they do, slant them as negatively as they can.

Art's power over Rockingham County is staggering but is very, very real. Bo will be working triple shifts just to live up to his obligations. Art has never taken such a scary approach toward anyone before, but it doesn't stop him from doing it now. Bo is the cheating, lying, stealing son-of-a-bitch trying to bring down Art's daughter.

With Art? . . .Ugh. . .**No.**

32

Game Day is here! Fans already pack the minor league-sized stadium just to watch batting practice. The scouts are there too. There are nearly two hours before game time. The Rookies play like they're already in the Big Leagues. The hitting, fielding and pitching perform in peak-point machination.

They are given a polite applause leaving the field but when the UNH Bob Cats enter the practice area, the bleachers practically rise from the standing ovation. The hitters are giving the fielders a good run around. Outfielders are shagging, infielders are scooping and there is no shortage of homeruns during batting practice.

With the legend preceding him, Sammy feels like he can sense eyeballs peering and searing through the numbers on his jersey. He begins playing catch with Jimmy. The fans around the bull pen cheer. Most in attendance assume that Sammy will start for the Bob Cats. A 'legend before his time' is quite applicable here. It couldn't be any closer to the truth. The stories, myths or not, spread like wildfire.

He begins taking signs from Jimmy, and the crowd sees it right away. Sammy throws a Slider, and then another pronator. Some folks in the stands gasp at the sight. Jimmy asks for a Knuckle-Curve. No one knows what to call it because they have never seen a real one before. And then? Pronator.

Sammy throws a series of Fastballs, certainly

the fastest ever seen outside of Fenway Park. Next come a series of Curveballs, and then a pronator answer for each. The loud murmur around him says people are looking, they are seeing, and they are understanding.

The Gyroball is a hard one to pick-up on but half the bull pen spectators can clearly see the strangest movements they've ever seen from a throw. Sammy pitches two Screwballs and two more pronators. Jimmy signs a series of Change-ups, then Sammy lobs a few Knuckle Balls in there. The fans are amazed.

Sammy and Jimmy end their practice with an astonishing show of Cutters; Up, down, left corners, right corners and nothing above the knees. Sammy and Jimmy towel down and then sit down on the bull pen bench. Their crowd is still cheering.

Sammy just sits still with his head down. He is humble that way, although when he is called back to the locker room, he tips, and then takes his hat off for all his fans.

McDowell and Seaver did not leave 'class' out of their lessons to Sammy and Jimmy.

The crowd cheers as the UNH Bob Cats take the field in the top of the first inning. There is also an undercurrent of question when the people realize Sammy isn't on the mound. And, that Jimmy is missing from behind the plate.

UNH starts against a giant size left-handed pitcher against a half-right, half-left BoSox Rookie batting order. He throws a mean Slider and unbelievable Sinker. He finishes with a moving Fastball at 98 MPH.

He strikes out the top of the order, all three with the same sequence. That gives him the confidence to pitch this game. He fully admits to himself that he was terrified on that mound that opening half-inning. He takes off his cap and towels down his head, face, neck and shoulders. The cap goes back on to stay for the rest of his game.

UNH gets a double at the top of the order but he was left standing there after an infield out, a strike out and fly out. At least they're getting some wood on the ball.

After five full innings, with a solo homerun each, the score is tied with one run a piece. In the top of the sixth, the BoSox Rookies begin with a deluge of base hits. The first batter strikes out but then, the next batter bounces a double over the wall.

The Rookies have picked-up on that sliding Fastball. A base hit brings the runner home. With a man on 1st and 2nd, the Rookies score again on a base hit. The score is 3-1 when the last batter grounds-out.

"Base-hits batters!" The UNH Manager calls, "Come on men, talk back to those Rookies."

UNH starts the bottom of the sixth with the top of the order. On the first pitch, the first batter hits a bullet up the first base line: A fair ball for a double. The next batter hits a line drive that drops into right field. UNH scores.

UNH has a man on second, with one out. Barfield, the clean-up man, takes two balls. He's looking for a Change-up, outside. Sure enough, this is the pitch that floats in. The line Coach gives him the 'hit away.' Barfield could have reached for it but why bother? At 3 and 0, here comes the Slider just above the knees, sweeping the plate. Barfield hits the ball so hard it appears able to unwrap the cowhide off the sphere, like a shot in that movie "The Natural."

At the top of the seventh, it's UNH 4 and

the BoSox Rookies 3. A growing roar from the crowd builds with a mad rush of excitement. The UNH Manager is walking back to the dugout after reviewing the roster with the plate umpire. Sammy and Jimmy are in!

The duo has a pitching sequence with locations all worked out for the upcoming batters. The Gyroball sails in and tricks the batter into swinging high. Sammy takes a big risk and gets as much sweat off his neck and forehead to sneak by a classic Spitball. He finishes off the third batter with a stinging and moving Two-Seam Fastball.

Sammy and Jimmy play with the next batter by starting him off with a Four-Seam Fastball, caught looking at a spec that looks like a hazelnut at 104 MPH. The bait is laid for Sammy to hook the big man with a big old hairy pronator Knuckle-Curve. This batter is convinced a Change-up is on its way next.

Sammy throws a 97 MPH Slider. It slices the plate diagonally and beats the swing.

"Yer out!" The plate ump calls.

The third batter in the inning represents the top of the lineup for the Rookies. Sammy throws a Gyroball with so much movement that all the batter can do is stand in the box with the bat on his shoulder.

"Fuck!" He yells and is given a warning by the umpire. Wittingly knowing the emotions are running high, Sammy winds-up right away and pitches a pronator Cutter. It is a little off-speed but effective as he gets a swing and a miss. Sammy smiles behind his mitt as he reads Jimmy's sign for a Knuckle Ball. It comes in breaking four times right to left and back, then just as it hits the outside corner, it simply drops right into Jimmy's basket like an over-ripe apple from an angry orchard. He tosses the ball toward the mound and trots to the dugout.

The bottom of the inning brings an electrifying first pitch hit that is heading over the center field wall until the Rookie Center Fielder runs to that wall and jumps five feet in the air to snatch it. It could not have been done any more eloquently. He wings the ball to the Shortstop and holds up a finger; one out!

Next inning, Jimmy steps into the batter's box and digs-in. He taps the plate a couple times and then gets set to take his stance. He takes a Fastball outside for a ball. He admits he let a homerun pitch get away. The Rookies' Pitcher throws an over-arching curve that got hung up high. Of course, it is off speed and gives Jimmy a good, long look at it. The ball comes in just above the letters, and away. Jimmy likes it. His bat audibly whips and meets the ball. The announcers call it out of there at that very second. And it is! A line-drive homerun puts the score at 5 to 3, UNH.

The Rookie Manager visits the mound, takes the ball from the pitcher's hand, and signals the bull pen for a left-hander. A tall slender Rookie trots up to the mound, has a few words with his manager and catcher, then takes his warm-up throws.

The remaining lineup is ready to go; the Shortstop steps into the batter's box. The first pitch comes, and he hits a single down the third base line. That was dangerously close to bring a double, even a triple.

The second baseman steps into the batter's box, cleats it around a little and waves his bat behind his head, kind of like "Yaz" used to do.

He swings and hits a Curveball to 2nd base, it's flipped to first for a 4/3 double-play.

The Pitch sequences and locations change from last inning. As the Rookie hitting Coaches scramble for a way to overcome Sammy Costello's pitching game, the UNH pitcher and catcher finalize their plans.

Sammy has yet to throw a Fastball. And he plans to use that to his advantage in this ninth inning. He knows the hitters are looking for movement, sometimes crazy movement. So, his first pitch is a Four-Seam Fastball. This pitch is the hardest of the Fastballs. It rotates backwards keeping the ball straight with no movement. It's straight down the lane, at 103 MPH, and a called strike. He gave away a dinger, but the hitter didn't swing. Strike one.

Jimmy signs for a Two-Seam Fastball-Sinker. The pitch is a Fastball that is just gripped differently than the Four-Seamer. It is held with the seams rather than across them. This pitch moves arm side of the pitcher and down. This movement is a result of the seams catching the air in a way that pushes the ball down and in to righties from a right-handed pitcher. But Sammy is throwing pronator, which causes the batter to swing like a clown and almost fall. It travels 6 to 8 MPH slower than the Four-Seamer.

A swing and a miss for strike 2.

Various baseball pitch grips, like the grip for a Slider, and other different types of pitches in Baseball are deceivingly similar. The Slider grip and Two-Seam Fastball are a good example. This is the same pitch as the Sinker, but some pitchers have trouble making the ball dive towards the ground. If the ball moves to the pitcher's arm side, inside to a righty from a right-handed pitcher, and doesn't have any depth, then the ball gets away. Although, Sammy has the pronator.

It's 4 to 6 MPH slower than the Four-Seamer. The Cut Fastball is one still in the Fastball family and moves the opposite way of the Two-Seamer. Sammy can augment the pitch using the pronator muscle. Out of the hand it looks a little like a 'cement mixer' Slider. With spin that is looser than a Slider, it can be tough to pick up the rotation early, because there is no red dot in the middle of the ball!

It has similar action to the Slider, just less movement. It also has more velocity than the Slider: 5 to 8 MPH slower than Four-Seamer. This pitch moves only a few inches to the pitcher's glove side and doesn't usually have much depth. Called strike three.

Knuckle-Curve grip used as a Slider glides at an angle towards the pitcher's glove side with depth. It's usually 9-12 MPH slower than the Four-Seam Fastball. You will see tight spin with a red dot, seams converging and spinning, to help identify the Slider. It usually has a break of 3-6 inches.

Curveballs have significantly more depth than the Slider, and usually have a 12-6 break as if looking at a clock. Spin is straight over the top, and the ball looks like it has a hump coming out of the pitcher's hand.

The Circle Change-up pitch is also a Knuckle-Curve and has the same movement as a regular Curve. The only difference is the grip and speed that is usually around 15 MPH slower than a Fastball. Every now and then, a pitcher will throw it harder but still not as hard as the Slider. . . Swung at and missed for Strike One.

A Slurve is a mixture of the Slider and Curveball. It is usually big and loopy, but its break angle is more of a 10-4 or 11-5 if looking at a clock, pitched from a righthander. It is closer to the Curveball speed than the Slider speed. The Slurve, and not many people know this, is more common than a true Curveball. Swing and a miss; Strike 2.

The Change-up is supposed to have the same spin as a Fastball but it's 6-9 MPH slower than the Fastball. Depending on the pitcher, some will throw a Change-up that has a little depth, and some just float it in there and rely on the change in speed, location, and the similar spin for effectiveness. Called Strike Three.

A Split-Finger can be thrown hard, or softer to act like a Change-up. Regardless of the velocity with which it is thrown the action is the same. There is a tumbling down action to the ball, which can be seen out of the pitcher's hand. The baseball is ready to take to Home plate. In the zone it dives into the dirt as it reaches the catcher. This pitch has very late down movement which makes it hard to lay off. Most times it is not thrown for a strike. It's used mostly as a strike-*out* pitch. But Sammy also uses them as filler pitches. Same with the Knuckle Ball.

Split-Finger Fastball grip and a Knuckle Ball are usually thrown very slow and used on almost every pitch. The ball comes into the zone with almost no rotation. This will make the ball flutter, having unpredictable movement which can make the pitch tough to hit and catch. The adage remains true when hitting a Knuckle Ball: 'If its high, let it fly; If its low, let it go.' Unless you can see the ball over the plate.

The lefty brought in last inning is on fire.

He's got a Four-Seam Fastball that moves. This intrigues Sammy as he watches from the bull pen. And the guy has a Cutter that crosses front corner to rear right at the knees. These pitches make his Change-up even more effective than most.

The Rookie strikes out batters two and five, and now faces one of the biggest men in the UNH lineup. He fouls away the Fastball but got a piece of it. He won't see that one coming at him anymore. He swings and misses the Cutter. Asking for time, he steps out of the batter's box for a moment. The pitcher is throwing consecutive sequences. Will he throw the Change-up?

The ump says, "Back in the box now, batter. Let's go."

Here it comes, as expected, and a welcome guest. The Change-up floats in slow but does not fool the batter. The ball is belt-high, and the bat is cocked and ready. He hits the longest ball today. It's going, going, and it is gone. It's gone out over the wall but out of the stadium!

"And someone in the parking lot has a souvenir!"

A ground out ends the eighth inning but only after that epic homerun brought the score to 6-3, UNH.

Sammy and Jimmy decide to goof-out the Rookies with their weirdest moving, or not, pitches. They mention nothing to their Manager, and while warming up just stay with Fastballs, Knuckle-Curves and Palm Ball Change-ups.

The first batter goes down with two Eephus droppers and a looping, rising and falling Gyroball.

The second batter goes down on two Gyroballs and a Knuckle Ball.

The third out comes by way of alternating pronator and back a Slurve, a Cutter and a Screwball.

"UNH score a walk-off!!"

"UNH score a walk-off!!"

33

The UNH-BoSox Rookie game puts a face to one "Sammy Costello," and puts the young pitcher on the world map. The sports sections everywhere, radio and other social media sports outlets have somebody new to bother. They try to compare his pitching to others of the past, but they can't. There has never been anyone like Sammy and no one remotely near him now; in style, diversity and in performance.

Media and the Press are given very limited access to the campus. Sammy leaves that cocoon at his own risk. He can practice on his own time, but his grades are low compared to last year. He tries practice at night and during the day, swapping classes from night to day and back. His Dad knows Sammy is struggling and is extremely anxious, so he steps into the situation.

Art, McDowell and Seaver meet for a teleconference to discuss Sammy's options.

"I think we ought to let him play: It's an open playing field right now." Tom Seaver suggests, and then continues. "He finishes school during off-time, or a full-time off-season."

"I like the off-season idea," McDowell says. "He can concentrate on the games *and* positions him well for college graduation in two years."

Art agrees and will meet Sammy and Jimmy at the Dean's office. The Dean is aware of the controversies and complications. He wants the young men to thrive on their talents, and to earn their degrees at UNH. The director's office creates for Art a covenant and negotiation that explains clearly the remaining college lives of Sammy Costello and Jimmy Presta.

Art rifles through letters of promise from nearly every team in MLB. He pulls out the packet from the Boston Red Sox. He replies to it stating that Sammy and Jimmy would rather play nowhere if not for Boston. The General Manager and Art escalate their conversations to telephone.

Boston wants a guarantee that the young men will finish schooling in due time. The team welcomes Sammy and Jimmy as walk-ons. They will be in a judgement-free area. The Red Sox will be prepared to discuss contracts and salary once or if the players make the cut. That's standard. Sammy and Jimmy are sticking with their Management, their Training and Team.

It's also standard for a star player to have and work with professional representation, typically in the form of an attorney and an agent. As the semester winds down at UNH, Art shops Sammy and Jimmy for the strongest delegation he can find. He calls and finishes one at a time. There will be no overlapping. The Scout Art picks speaks for the Red Sox. He will provide the details of Sammy's and Jimmy's scouting reports.

Behind the conference room doors, the BoSox don't underplay their pining for Sammy. He's obviously diligent, focused, determined, strong and fit, and clean and healthy. He also knows tricky pitches most have never heard of, and of course, he spent years of his childhood learning and implementing the pronator muscle.

This kid accomplished all that on his own. He shows patience all through Little League, Babe Ruth League, High School Ball and UNH Pitching. His Coaches include Tom Seaver and Sam McDowell, along with his Art. Now, the chance to have such a young man of great and intelligent talent and integrity on our side; on our roster; in our bull pen; starter, reliever or closer; and winning lots of games for us is something to live up to!

Of course, outside those doors the execs try their best to play it cool, like it's no big deal. They fool no one. The only line item leaked about Sammy so far is that his salary doubles after earning his college degree. Scholastic incentive done the easy way. Jimmy gets the same deal.

The minimum salary is the lowest amount

which a club can pay a player for a full season in the Major Leagues. Its amount is set in the Collective Bargaining Agreement. In the CBA, the minimum Major League Baseball salary was raised by 50% to $300,000. This figure was 291% higher than a full-time salary based on the U.S. Federal Minimum Wage but still a pittance compared to the average MLB salary, which was $12,300,000 million previously. The minimum salary has grown tremendously over the past three decades. It was set at $150,000 per year in the 1973 Collective Bargaining Agreement and reached $400,000 a few years later. It takes another big jump with the conclusion of a new CBA effective in the late 1970s. A minimum salary is also set for the various classes of Minor Leagues in organized Baseball.

Only a minority of players are paid the minimum salary at any given time, but most players will be paid at that level at *some* point of their careers. Almost all players are paid the minimum salary as rookies. The exception is the few very high draft choices or international free agents who can negotiate a higher initial rate of pay, with proper representation. The minimum is also paid to players who have failed to establish themselves for a full year in previous major league stints. Players who have been released by another team are forced to accept the minimum to sign-on with another team.

Teams also must pay the minimum salary to a player who has been released by another team which is still responsible for paying his salary for the remainder of the season. After the season has started, Team A releases a player making $1 million for the year; it is responsible for paying that salary and any future guaranteed years. If Team B signs the player, it only needs to pay the prorated amount of the yearly minimum salary to the player, with Team A still responsible the remaining portion.

Scouting, Legal, Agency Representation and Art have a lot to work with, such as all the Scouting live and machine output, realistic base pay for all the value Sammy represents. Add to that all the specificities of Sammy's work ethic and gentlemanly ways Art and Sammy bring. They must quantify all that and much more to money that will have been made by Sammy for himself, sure but more so generated for the team, management and owners especially!

The Management Office would like to watch and see Sammy pitch three rounds to the Red Sox starting lineup. There is a twenty-minute break between each round. Management has all the motion, speed and video machines running.

Their Scout tells them they're almost missing the show without watching the full pitches, windup through the catch but it's up to them. Fucking lazy management. Fucking machines. All the same.

Several grey suits simply do not want to witness their best hitters go down. Sammy and Jimmy take their time beforehand to outline their pitching sequences and locations for each batter, and then completely turn things inside-out the second time through. The third time through is their chance to have some fun and blow management away, along with the batters.

They manage the first round without trickery by pronator. They used the second round to exploit the pronator. No one there has ever seen so many stumbling, off-balance batters. The batters are so worn out that Sammy and Jimmy use a sample MLB pitch sequence and location menu to easily hold the third-round hitters down.

All present are utterly speechless: The batters, the scout and legal representation, the team and management, are all so amazed that they finally understand. They have some decisions to make. Sammy and Jimmy ease off the field and into the locker room showers.

GAME ON

34

According to a leak from the office, Sammy receives an eight-year contract with the Boston Red Sox. There are generous options at contract end for both sides. No salary amounts are made public. Whether Sammy signs is not made public. Knowledge, guesses, speculation and arguments about his pitching break out all over baseball country, and even in Japan. Sammy makes sure Jimmy is well taken care of, too, and hits the exceptional ceiling salary.

The New York Yankees pitch a double-amount salary personally to Art. He'll get it to

Sammy's Reps if all seems fit. The Sammy-Squad hold on to it, just to give NY a bit of agita from the waiting and false hope.

The preseason and exhibition BoSox games sell out. Watching Sammy is like watching the young Mike Tyson fights; All over so fast but you *don't* want to miss a second of the action.

Pitching Coaches start Sammy no more than once a week, or one game out of five. The Sox are leery and cautious of Sammy's arm. They must acclimate their trainers on the pronator. He takes all his usual pitching practice with Jimmy but they both also join the team for jogs and calisthenics. When speaking of the situations coming and going between the duo and the team pitching Coaches, they agree on the handholding.

"They think they're doing something good." Jimmy says. "They'll get over it."

"With all your baker's dozen or more solid pitches and adding the pronator option for most of them, the pitching coach says, "Keeping in shape in support of the team is necessary for your pitching and catching practice, least be said."

"Working through our menu is quite a workout but well worth the time and effort if I expect to be dependent on any single one of them." Sammy confirms.

"Sammy is exactly right, Coach." Jimmy offers.

"I can't come up with one pitch or a variation of, that you don't already throw. You are the weapon of choice. I'm sure you know that. But please do continue the team workouts. They'll help you stay generally strong and feed you longevity. Plus, the other players like to see you out there. . .with them. You know?"

"Yes, sir." Sammy and Jimmy say. "We'll keep up with it."

"Thanks fellas. You're a really good couple of strong, young men, and I'm proud to coach you."

"Thanks a lot, Coach."

"Any word out yet on the opening day's starter?" Jimmy asks.

"No, not yet, Jimmy. I believe the Skipper wants it to remain a mystery until that day comes."

"Is that out of the ordinary for the Sox?"

"I'd have to say, generally, no. But you two stirred into the stew may be leaning him one way then the other."

"Are you kidding?"

"Well, come on, you know he wants to play

head games with all the other teams." The Coach laughs with the squad as he walks away.

It's nice and warm in Winter Haven, Florida, and Sammy and Jimmy spend more time than usual out in the park. Sammy has an idea.

"Hey Jimmy, let's get our girls down here today!" Access to anyone in the organization is not easy but today is open.

"I heard of a place close by. We can go and swim with the manatees! They all swim around the dock that's there. We can feed them, too, if you want. You just slip into the water and you're with them; the puppies of the sea. The girls will love it!

"Call Norma and have her tell Catherine. Just repeat what I just told you."

"The most fun yet down here in South Florida!" Sammy cries out.

Personal relationships are near impossible to keep propped up with the League maintaining each member of the organization up to League standards, restrictions and regulations. Catherine and Norma have been with Jimmy and Sammy, albeit hot and cold in the beginning, for over four years. The couples are clearly in love now, with no lack of honor and trust. The weddings are planned and celebrated.

The girls have the idea down pat. They understand that the League sometimes comes between them and their guys. Their answer, usually fun and loud is:

"It's *all* for *ball!*"

Period.

They live comfortably and close by, always going out to do something or another, like shopping, brunch, movies, and personal visits to or from their men. Today is extra special:

"Swimming with the manatees!"

The girls park at the field and hop in with the guys to go to the marina. There is a chart that describes certain aspects of the sea cows.

"Hey you guys," Jimmy says. "I'm going to read these facts about Manatees. You should listen."

"Oh God. . .Typical Jimmy. . .Has to know all the facts." Norma replies with a chuckle, along with Catherine and Sammy.

"COMMON NAME: Manatees;

"SCIENTIFIC NAME: Trichechus;

"TYPE: Mammals;

"DIET: Herbivores;

"AVERAGE LIFE SPAN IN THE WILD: 40 years;

"SIZE: 8-13 feet;

"WEIGHT: 440-1,300 pounds;

"Now, about Manatees:

"Manatees are sometimes called sea cows, and their languid pace lends merit to the comparison.

"Aquatic Life:

"Despite their massive bulk, they are graceful swimmers in coastal waters and rivers. Powering themselves with their strong tails, manatees typically glide along at 5 miles an hour but can swim 15 miles an hour in short bursts.

"Manatees are usually seen alone, in pairs, or in small groups of a half dozen or fewer animals. From above the water's surface, the animal's nose and nostrils are often the only thing visible. Manatees never leave the water but like all marine mammals, they must breathe air at the surface. A resting manatee can remain submerged for up to 15 minutes but while swimming it must surface every three or four minutes.

"Manatee Populations:

"There are three species of manatee, distinguished primarily by where they live. The West Indian manatee ranges along the North American east coast from Florida to Brazil. The Amazonian manatee species inhabit the Amazon River and the African manatee swims along the west coast and rivers of Africa.

"Parenting and Diet:

"Manatees are born underwater. Mothers must help their calves to the surface so that they can take their first breath, but the infants can typically swim on their own only an hour later.

"Manatee calves drink their mothers' milk, but adults are voracious grazers. They eat water grasses, weeds, and algae, and lots of them. A manatee can eat a tenth of its own massive weight in just 24 hours.

"Threats to Survival:

"Manatees are large, slow-moving animals that frequent coastal waters and rivers. These attributes make them vulnerable to hunters seeking their hides, oil, and bones. Manatee numbers declined throughout the last century, mostly because of hunting pressure. Today, manatees are at-risk. Though protected by laws they still face threats of extinction.

"The gentle beasts are often accidentally hit by motorboats in ever more crowded waters and sometimes become entangled in fishing nets."

"Ahhh. Ohhh shit." Norma sorrowfully says.

"OK. Got it! I'm going in. Look at all of them over here." Catherine says.

"I'm in, too!" answers Norma.

Sammy and Jimmy lean over the edge of the dock and pet the sea cows as they swim or float by.

"Come on, guys!" Catherine calls out.

"Yeah, come on in!" Norma speaks up.

"OK," Sammy says. "Let's join the crowd."

"Right behind you." Jimmy says.

The two couples stay in with the puppies, as they call the manatees, over three hours. Norma notices that Jimmy is beet-red and suggests he take cover, because he's clearly gotten too much sun.

Catherine looks at Sammy and tells him he's going to hurt. He is as red as a steamed Maine lobster.

She adds, "You'll be lucky to get the uniform on, let alone perform any movement in it at all. . .hate to say it."

The girls wear one-piece suits and use heavy doses of sun screen on the exposed skin. Always thinking. Just not thinking of their guys quite as early this time.

"I hope you don't get in trouble." Norma says.

"Oh, we will," Sammy says. "Leave it all for now. Jimmy and I will handle it."

35

"Long sleeve light linen white tee, white cap, white lightweight running pants, or jams," the Coach says, then raises his voice. "Both of you!" He laughs. "Fucking numb nuts. Sheesh."

"Let's just throw easy for a while." Sammy says. "I feel I can hardly move right now."

"See how things go, yeah." Jimmy agrees.

They are excused from the daily calisthenics but join the team for their jog. The rumor mill is abuzz with speculative personal business of Sammy, and Jimmy, too, like favoritism. But Sammy is who everybody is talking most about. All they need do to sober up is to call up the memory of going down on strikes three times in a row against Sammy a few days ago.

Men never grow up or out of it: Money. Thinking of it becomes maddening and an annoyance. For others, likewise the vets, it holds no weight whatsoever to drag around with them. They are smart in their ways in the ways in The Show.

"Try to keep your minds on the game," Naz says, as the team listens to their big dark-skinned Team Captain.

"Moreover, for the good of the team. Have you ever seen a pitcher like that boy Sammy? **No.** Could you hit him? **No.** So, let's be respectful, here, guys. Be glad he's on *our* side! Besides, no one is qualified to judge anyone else."

Off-season, Sammy wins 20 games. They were all by way of shut outs, including eleven no-hitters. Teams everywhere have analysts dissecting every move grip and spin they can capture. And naturally that damn pronator muscle movement.

They tend to forget the squad Sammy had growing up, with Jimmy, his Dad Art, Sam McDowell, Tom Seaver and the rest. They are ignorant of the facts that Sammy practiced every day. He put in over two hours throwing with pitching in mind, plus fielding and hitting workouts with his Dad. He was dedicated and committed from the age of seven years old. He proves it every day.

"Grow-up! And have fun with it!" Naz raises his voice. *"Watch what he does to our opposing hitters. HAHA Y'all just wait!"*

The cuts and drafts day nears, which nerve wracks everyone, like they are wearing red targets on their backs. The vets know, you take nothing for granted. Changes are made for the wrong reasons as well as for good ones. Even contractors aren't strictly safe. It's no wonder that the 'loudest' men wearing a Boston uniform this Spring are the most quiet and peaceful young men on the team.

The owners and management convene in NYC for the conventionalism and politesse. The movements are done on Sunday. All the finalities occur here, live on television. Most team heads walk away happy, although there is always some bit of hot bidding and bartering. Complaining. Arguments.

Each team announces the players they are bringing up from the farm. The Minor Leagues grow and become stronger every season, which makes it difficult for owners to decide who stays in and who they take out. Players are dismissed from this weekend through the end of the week. They will meet next weekend to learn their fate.

Sammy and Jimmy decide to stay at camp housing and take a well-deserved rest. Their girls treat them like kings. They know tensions are running high. They are aware of Sammy's and Jimmy's talent but have no idea what can come from the cut and draft event. They know enough about Baseball superstitions that no one mentions *anything* until *after* it happens or culminates. And there is no speaking of anything jinx-related either! Jinxing and superstition is still alive and well in Major League Baseball.

Boston is bringing up a Rookie Catcher from Class A. They plan to promote all other younger players from within, as called for. Their starting roster stays the same yet with decent, talented backups and 2nd stringers. The subject of talk at the convention that is mysteriously absent: Sammy Costello and Jimmy Presta.

The top floor conference suite across the street at the Hyatt is all set up for the private Boston Red Sox management meeting. Boston's Owners, Management, the young players' Legal Representation and Agents, Tom, Sam and Art sip on Laphroaig and chat over the comings and goings of the weekend. There are several very big boys coming up: They can hit hard. There is a Shortstop who is one man of magic hands.

They in attendance know what they are there for, and they fish small paper pads and pencils from their interior suit coat pockets. An owner writes something down, tears the page out and slides it face down across the coffee table to the Rep.

The Rep lifts the edge and glances at the numbers he sees there. They trade the writing paper like dealers and players at a Vegas Black Jack Table. This part of the negotiation is just the high-end deal-making; that is term and salary.

Following that agreement, the discussion is based purely on merit, strengths, talent and further potential. They consider attendance, merchandising, which will be huge, the press and all the media they'll attract. Sammy's personal representatives attending hold a quiet, 20-minute, low-key sidebar discussion at the other end of the room.

When they are done, Sammy's Agent makes the announcement:

"$18,000,000 per year guaranteed salary.

"Monetary amount doubles after Master Costello earns his college degree.

"Eight-year initial term with end time

options, good for both sides, with a fair variable-year term.

Payday Direct Deposits into Mr. Samuel Costello's Bank and Investment Companies on the 15th and 29th of each month.

30% to Bank/Money Market;

70% to Investment, currently with Fidelity.

"First Year Salary to be delivered upfront in one lump sum, 50-50 into the Bank and Investment institutions: They are established and aware of their responsibilities.

Missus Catherine Costello's and Sammy's bank cards will each be fortified by $10,000.00 on the first of every month. It is to be their disposable income. These are not cumulative funds. Every month, any balance is transferred back to the source, bank or investment, and the prepaid card will be refilled.

The Prestas request the same arrangements for Jimmy Presta at $10,000,000 a year.

Art Costello works aside the Bank and Investment Agencies to make sure the boys are well taken care of and that the money continues to grow and accumulate in both depositaries. The Presta family is happy to have Art overseeing Jimmy's funds, as well.

36

Sammy and Jimmy decide to go in on bonuses for their entire squad, including Art and Sophia, Tom, Sam, the Scout, the Rep, and the Attorney. Tom and Sam try to refuse it, but Sammy wouldn't hear of it.

"No way. For all you did for us, you're taking our gift to you!"

Handwritten notes on the inside of each card state that "Please: No one share the amount or what you receive with anybody else." It also simply states, "Jimmy and I worked a long time on this, and you helped us through it. Keep your bonus to yourself, and, for yourself. Enjoy!

"THANK YOU VERY MUCH," signed Sammy Costello and Jimmy Presta.

Art and Sophia, Tom, Sam, the Scout, the Rep, and the Attorney each receive a Cashier's Check for an $150,000.

Without reading out loud, Art reads to himself that Sammy went a little further with his good fortune. He gives $75,000 to Anita. He adds to the same card and message he gave the others, plus, above his signature, "All my love to my sister, Anita. Please create a college fund for you and your little one. Accept help from Dad with your money management."

In an odd card, Art reads to himself that Sammy reached out to a person he respected and who got screwed by his sister Tristy. He gives $25,000 to Doug, his ex-brother-in-law. He adds to the same card and message he gave the others, and just above his signature. "Doug, you've always been a good guy to me. Best, Sammy."

In the last envelope with the same card with the pre-printed instruction, is a check for $5,000 for Tristy. It is without any extra or personalized note or signature. Just his name.

Boston is down to their final week of Spring Training. Opening Day, and the first series of the year, they will host the Oakland Athletics at Fenway Park. The players take Monday through Wednesday off to enjoy their families. They report to the park Thursday for a full-on practice and several speeches by the Owners, Managers and Coaches. Game 1 is Friday night. Game 2 is Saturday afternoon, and Game 3 is on Sunday afternoon. Jimmy studies the 'Pitcher's Limitation by Pitch' chart.

Sammy learns from his Coach that he will start Sunday's game, third of three in the series.

The tall skinny man reaches high up on his toes. He extends further back as far as he can go on the closet shelf. He's got it. He is soothed by the soft, supple leather that wraps the case all around. He shuffles a few items around, so he can get what he wants down from, and out of there. He is more than anxiously frustrated as the sweat drips into his eyes, stinging. It drips down from his nose and his chin, his ears and onto his hairless chest.

Ah, there. He's got it. He lays it on the bed and opens it up, like it is a cherished treasure. Perhaps to him it is. He towel dries it and then returns to the bedroom. He looks at it and smiles with a look of love. He runs his fingertips up and down, and back and forth on each piece, like it's a real woman he wishes to please.

He admires the brown barley tanning over the leather case and the contrast to the sand and brown camouflage on the pieces. Even though he hasn't touched her in years, he still loves her. He strokes her. He gently closes the case and slips it inside his built-in headboard cubby.

With opening season upon them, Red Sox fans scoop up the tickets. He is a big fan but can't afford a season ticket. So, he responds to every open Fenway Park job that's out there. Food and Beverage, Usher, Ticket Taker, Security, Clean-up Crew, Park Maintenance, Field Marker and Game Prep. He goes to Boston to apply and then grabs his beautifully encased and raised custom cue for a few racks at a pub he knows of a couple blocks from Fenway.

Sammy and Jimmy practice their default pitch sequences and locations every day. They also practice their crazy pitch sequence and finally the "Sure Strike Three" pitches. So, this sequence, with or without the pronator options, produce batter outs. By strike, either called or swinging, or by ground ball.

1. Gyroball -- like an analog wave floating up and falling all the way to the plate; a magic pitch; gets in a batter's mind who thinks it's rising when it's dropping.

2. Spitball -- just a few beads of sweat off his eyebrow give Sammy's Spitball an

oblong bubble that no one has ever hit. No one ever says a thing.

3. Two-Seam Fastball -- this is one *fast* Fastball but unlike the Four-Seam, this one that *does* move as it reaches the plate. It's a strike or an out.

4. Slurve -- a mixture of the Slider and Curveball. Usually big and loopy but its break angle is more of a 10-4 or 11-5 if looking at a clock.

5. Knuckle-Curve -- it's like a Curveball on steroids. It's nearly unhittable.

6. Slider -- It's fast and it moves. It's a strike three pitch.

7. Cutter -- It perplexes everyone that this isn't number one. The wonders of this pitch are that you think it is a Fastball, then, *wonk*, it breaks away. It literally

tricks that hitter; looks like a Fastball but then, it moves.

8. Knuckle Ball -- It will break big 3 or 4 times before reaching the plate. Keep it coming in low and it's a strike-out pitch. Leave one high, and you're serving up a Meatball to your hungry batter.

Oakland loses by three runs Friday night. Then, they come back and beat Boston 2-1 on Saturday afternoon. Sunday afternoon is a gorgeous day for baseball. The breeze is easy as everybody there is 'wound up' with Sammy on the 'mound up!'

He and Jimmy work through the lineup using the pitching sequences and locations they practiced for two days. They throw more pronator pitches than originally planned but there is no consequence. It is just a small tweak in the battleplan. They shut out the Athletics, 3-0.

Boston is on the road and on their way to play the White Sox and then the Indians. There are three games with each team scheduled this nine-day road trip, then they'll be home again.

Sammy and Jimmy let their Coach know they plan to change their typical pitching sequence, though not necessarily location. They want to try mixing in more Breakers and Change-ups.

They demo the sequences for the Pitching Coach. Both Jimmy and Sammy look forward to the day when they will no longer have to walk through their menu of the game each time.

Sammy talks through the menu:

"Curveball -- Virtually every pitcher in the League has a Curveball;

"Split-finger Fastball (Splitter) -- Splitters are great pitches. They brake enough to get any batter out with the proper location. Just look at a nicely thrown Splitter. The Splitter spin on the ball is nearly invisible;

"Screwball -- Curls like a pigtail and we can make it go either way with my pronator muscles;

"Knuckle Ball -- Tricky pitch, although it's prone to be hit for homers if left up in the zone. Otherwise, it's very hard to hit. It's a truly well-rounded pitch. It breaks big three or four times on the way to the plate;

"Cutter -- You think it is a Fastball, then, *bam,* it breaks away. It'll strike batters out 9 out of 10 times. It really tricks that hitter looking like a Four-Seam Fastball, but it moves;

"Eephus Pitch -- This pitch really drops

on the batter and looks like a clown pitch; best used on heavy hitters. It can be thrown in the 40s. Really can mess up the hitters expecting a Fastball;

"12-6 Curveball -- It is a nasty roundhouse and it's easy to throw. This Curveball has significantly more depth than the Slider. It usually has a 12-6 break (as if looking at a clock). Spin is straight over the top, and the ball will look like it has a hump coming out of the pitcher's hand;

"Foshball -- Very much like a Splitter but with some tail away from a right-handed batter. Downright nasty pitch but very underrated, and rarely seen;

"Vulcan Change-up & Circle Change-up -- This is an amazing pitch combination, a cross between a Change-up and a Sinker. Besides the Eephus, it's the only Sinker on the menu;

"Slider -- This pitch slides at an angle towards the pitcher's glove side (depending on pronator) with depth. It's usually 9-12 MPH slower than the Four-Seam Fastball. You will see tight spin with a red dot (seams converging and spinning) to help you identify the Slider. It usually has a break of 3-6 inches;

"Change-up -- Is supposed to have the same spin as a Fastball but is 8-15 MPH slower than a Fastball. Depending on the pitcher, some will throw a Change-up that has a little depth, and some just float it in there and rely on the change of speed, and the similar spin for effectiveness;

"Split-Finger Fastball -- This can be thrown hard or softer to act like a Change-up. Regardless of the velocity it is thrown, the action is the same. The ball starts in the zone but then dives straight into the ground.

This pitch has very late down movement which makes it hard to lay off. Most times, it is not thrown for a strike. It's used mostly as a strike-*out* pitch."

Both Jimmy and Sammy again repeat the wish for the day when they will no longer have to walk through their menu of the game. And that was just a partial one!

37

He carries his case to work every day, and always invites others to join him for a rack and an ale afterward. He gets the Fenway Park aisle clean-up job in sections 34 through 43, in the right field bleachers; and 37 and 38, the upper bleacher. He even discovers a private little place to sit where he can see the whole game; every player.

His work begins postgame as soon as the sections are empty but also takes a pregame idiot-walk through his sections to make sure they are debris and garbage-free and the seats are clean and dry.

He accepts that job to keep throughout the Red Sox season but stays on for all Fenway Park events, like concerts and Monster Truck Rallies. Whatever the event, he is working it. It's so much easier since renting the studio apartment just around the corner from the ballpark. He chooses a monthly lease.

Truth be told he despises this skanky fucking job, but he'll be elsewhere before too long. He keeps his case to his left next to the seat. Reaching down and touching the leather comforts him. It is pacifying to the touch. His treatment gets rougher whenever Naz or Jimmy are at the plate.

He can see Art and his guests in their skyboxes right across the field. He experiences an involuntary reaction to hawk one up and spit every time he sees him; the son-of-a-bitch.

"Well looky here, motherfucker, I've got power, too. I can spy on you."

Art's group is going off on the Yankees. They can't wait to let Sammy loose on them. It's a five-game series, and Art is already thinking that Sammy can start the first and third or fourth games, and close the bottom of the fifth game, if necessary. He'll have to talk to the Skipper about all that, just to see.

Boston has two home series in a row. Everybody likes that; the fans, the players, and of course, their wives, girlfriends and families. The electrified city called Beantown is ready for another Sammy Costello performance. The Orioles are in town this week. They've got first place in the Division by two games over Boston.

Baltimore is in town for three-night games. They lose the first game by two runs in a shutout with Sammy on the mound. The fans absolutely adore him, and love watching him pitch. Baltimore won the last game by one run. If they lose one more and Boston wins just one, the Red Sox jump into 1st place in the Division.

After the third game against Baltimore on Wednesday, Sammy is relieved and ready to recline at home with Catherine. They decide to order in over the next two days. Chinese sounds good on Thursday, and it is, as always. They choose Café 1010 for a gourmet experience on Friday mid-afternoon, brought directly to them.

During his time at home, Sammy and Catherine make love like they are on an extension of their honeymoon. Sammy is mesmerized by his wife's beauty and sexuality. She is the sweetest, most generous female he has ever known, with her fine disposition and temperament. They've never felt more in love. She knows he's a superstar, but he doesn't act like one. She likes that more than anything else about him. He is humble and modest. For her, those are the sexiest things about him. She'd love him whether he was a star or not.

"So, Catherine," Sammy says. "I'll be pitching Game Two and Game Five. You should come to Game Five. The crowd will be up and loud the whole time."

"If that is what you wish babe, I'll be there on Friday."

"After the game will be much easier to handle on Friday. A lot of people will be hanging around for autographs. . .you know. . .and the street, meet and greet. Maybe we can sneak away after a little bit."

The phone rings. "Oh, hey Dad," Sammy answers. "What's up?"

"Do you have any guests for the skybox on Friday?" Art asks.

"Um, yeah, Dad. Put us down for Catherine Costello and Norma Presta, plus two."

"Ok. Good deal."

"Yeah. Jimmy's wife and another couple girls for your guys to ogle over." They have a laugh.

Tristy and Doug finally move to a Northeast New Jersey self-sufficient and self-sustained grove of small village homes in a place called Free Acres. It is hardly free to live there, ownership or not. Land cannot be acquired but the structures may be. Regulation station. For a short while the settling life seems like heaven.

'Wow. . .we live in Free Acres!'

But way too soon in their existence together, Doug falls into the habit of returning home from work, reclining and reading his books. It's all he wants to do; cares to do; wind-down.

Tristy hastily comes not only to despise the behavior but the man, as well. She wants to go out, go into The City, take day trips to Pennsylvania Water Gap and take vacations back up to New England, *do things*. Doug wants nothing to do with any of it, except the occasional vacation. They've already done it all. Doug works extra hours and extremely hard all day and wants to rest at night. He has survived two gun-to-head bank heists.

She refuses to try to understand his point of view, but he says he sees hers. He doesn't change, though. With a four-year-old daughter and an infant daughter, Tristy starts seeing someone else in place of her

husband. Of course, Doug discovers this --
he isn't blind -- so he moves out to a small
cottage at the other end of Free Acres. Nice
cottage and close to his kids.

Tristy moves her boyfriend into the house
with her; a bisexual, narcissistic spoiled guy
who just begs, many agree, for a smack in the
mouth. But for the sex, they have nothing.
He abuses her emotionally and verbally. But
they go places. They 'do things!' Tristy gets
her wish at the price of her family; namely
her little girls. She is as spoiled as her
boyfriend and as she's behaved all her life.

38

The seating cleaner faces even more trash than usual whenever the Yankees show up. There will be no pool tonight. After the preclean, he tucks into his little protective cage. He'll go once more to the men's room, then he's in to stay. He has *got* to see Sammy Costello pitch!

The young pitcher makes a quick jog from the bull pen to the mound. Thousands are already on their feet, cheering and screaming for him.

"How the fuck can he stand that!?"

But Sammy and Jimmy are both silently at

ease. They even thrive on taking on talent. But the Yankees are a bit more than that. Quite literally, they are the best team money can buy. It has always come down that way.

Sammy catches the first batter looking with a Knuckle-Curve. He then serves up what seems to be a straight down the lane Four-Seam Fastball; at least it looks like one, so the batter decides to swing. The ball comes in, just a little outside but then it cut. And it cut fast and hard across the plate. That's a swing and a miss.

Jimmy calls for what Sammy already wants to throw: A Change-up. Then Jimmy signs a Gyroball. The batter watches the red bead go up and down and in at the knees. No swing. No one has hit that pitch yet this season. The ump asks for the ball. He's studying it, dissecting it like it's a frog in a High

School biology project. The ump even becomes bored at the one-sidedness of the game.

Sammy throws a three-hitter for a BoSox win. He receives a standing ovation, turns, standing up high, head high then straight-arm points at Jimmy, and they both lift their caps. If anything, the fielders must remain twice as alert, since so few hits come their way, they must be ready when they do! Boston Fans, and Sammy Fans stand at their seats and applaud until every Red Sox player has left the field.

Chatter from every locker and coming through the showers is high level in the Yankee's locker room. For the first time in his career, the Manager has nothing to say. Not a word. He appears to be in shock, in a daze.

"It really is true. Everything they say about that kid is true! Shit!"

The players are cleaned and dressed, just hanging around, waiting for a word or two from their Manager, or a dismissal.

"Gentlemen, it really is true. Everything they say about that kid is true. Damn nice we don't have to face him again tomorrow. Ha! But he'll be back before this series ends. Meet here tomorrow for practice but be prepared to also spill your guts on dealing with him. Go home fellas. Try to relax."

The Yankees pull off a tight win the following night at three to two. Naz hits two solo Homeruns for the Red Sox. The Yankees' pitching is not that tough, but their fielding is amazing, and the lineup contains a few heavy hitters, and what's more, a lineup of sharp base-hitters.

So far, as of now, 'No' is known to be

the token answer; no gun made entirely of plastic is currently available. The closest thing is probably something like the Glock 17, an Austrian-made automatic pistol that has some plastic parts, including the grip and trigger guard. Training is required to recognize a disassembled Glock on an X-ray scanner. But it's still 83% metal by weight.

Are all-plastic weapons even feasible? Some think it's only a matter of time. Congress's Office of Technology Assessment reports that a 99% percent nonmetallic gun might someday be made using composite plastics, with metal used only for springs. A small Florida company called Red Eye Arms claims it is going to have a prototype plastic grenade launcher ready in 18-24 months.

Congress gets so spooked by the publicity about plastic weapons, even theoretical ones, that it bans their production in the United

States. Whether that scares off Red Eye or they were just hustling the gun industry equivalent of vaporware no one knows but the company can't be located now.

But who's to say what they're up to in those secret government labs? An issue of Modern Gun magazine carries an article entitled 'The CIA's Glass Gun,' with the arch subhead, 'The Agency Could Tell You About It. Its Amazing Ceramic Fully Automatic Pistol. But then, of Course, They'd Have to Kill You.' The article is sketchy, without sources, no quotes, and no indication how the information was obtained.

An editor's note says the gun in the accompanying photos is "a full-sized model made up for this article." The CIA declines to help. Strange. "Modern Gun," published by Larry Flynt, of Hustler magazine fame, calls itself "Entertainment for Gun Owners." This is perhaps not the world's most reliable source. Still, one tall skinny man does want to consider all the possibilities.

The article implies that the CIA made several prototype nonmetallic guns using a 'super hard ceramic material' originally developed for the exhaust valves in General Motors auto engines. The stuff 'literally has the strength of steel,' the article reads. One quote reads, "The agency considers the material so important to national security that it reportedly has its formula classified, thereby preventing GM from marketing it."

The gun depicted is a small automatic pistol, and a magazine of bullets loaded into the handle. When you pull the trigger, a plastic spring drives the bolt/slide mechanism forward, pushing a bullet from the magazine into the chamber and firing it. The bullet has no full metal jacket, and apparently is the loose equivalent of a small cannonball or musket with a powder charge behind it. The propellant ignites in two stages to keep the chamber pressure low enough that the gun doesn't blow up in your hand. The bullet itself can be ceramic or some aluminum/plastic composite.

The Glass Gun's 'asse,' its innovative material, also creates legal problems for the CIA," the article reads. "The Geneva Accords forbid the use by a nation's armed forces of anything but full metal casing ammunition, and except for the aluminum bullets, no part of the new gun or its ammunition is metallic. To save the Glass Gun project, Agency advocates argue to a Pentagon oversight committee that the Agency was civilian, not military, and the gun would be used by civilians."

The article goes on to say that counterterrorism, not assassination, is the goal of the nonmetallic pistols. Terrorists and foreign governments protecting terrorists use metal detectors just like we do; an agent underfriction gun with a glass gun could get past magnetometer security into an area where hostages are being held and proceed to shoot the bad guys.

Is this legit? An attempt to reach the editor of Modern Gun is unsuccessful, so the CIA is phoned. The CIA does have somebody in charge of public relations. Her job is to tell people no more than 'no comment,' which is exactly what she does. Next stop? GM. They say they don't use ceramics in engine valves anymore because it isn't cost-effective. Yes, but what about the CIA using GM material to make guns?

"You'd better ask the CIA about that."

Uh huh.

The Bureau of Alcohol, Tobacco, and Firearms

says, "we don't know," but the CIA is exempt from the federal law banning nondetectable guns. So, who knows? Maybe there really is a nonmetallic gun to be manufactured. Especially when it must only be good for two rounds

"That's all I need."

The invention is a nonmetallic gun barrel having a longitudinally rigid tubular exterior capable of radial elastic deformation upon passage of a projectile therethrough. Liner segments fixed at the inner diameter of the barrel exterior are abutted end to end and form spiraled rifling structures comprised of shallow channels and ridges. Radial gaps between sides of the liners can be partly filled by radial projections of elastomeric material of the barrel exterior. The radial projections expand inwardly to seal against a projectile bearing against the inner periphery of the barrel as the projectile is fired from the barrel.

He orders every part and piece he needs to assemble his own, one of a kind, non-metallic firearm. It is modeled after a Henry AR-7 Survival Rifle, with not a bit of metal. Having been a Field Artillery veteran, he has the confidence he needs to build out his collapsible, non-metallic rifle.

39

The Yankees beat the Red Sox in game two, 7-4. The Sox take Game Three, 4-3, as Naz hits a Grand Slam in the bottom of the Eighth. New York brings up a strong reliever with two on and two out. He walks the next batter, as his Manager throws his cap to the ground. His reliever is supposed to assure their win with a save!

Naz takes his time in the batter's on-deck circle. Swinging weighted bats, tarring his own, he cocks back and swings seven or eight times. He rubs dirt into his glove palms. He takes his helmet off and refits it on his head several times.

"Batter up!" The umpire yells. They get testy near the end of a game. They just want to get out of there and get home. "what're 'ya doin' over there? Jeezum H."

"Got to do my thing here Ump!" Naz laughs. "You want me to do good, now don't you?"

"Get in the box and then do something good." The ump is chuckling now. Sometimes he feels like a grade school teacher.

The pitcher doesn't want to walk a run in, and he doesn't want Naz to connect either. He puts one low and outside. Naz takes it for a ball. Next strike gets him swinging hard at a soft breaker. Ball speed gets him. Naz steps out, knocks dirt off his cleats, stretches out his jersey, adjusts his cup, and steps back in as he pushes his helmet tighter.

Naz points his bat at the Sox runners on first, second and then third. The catcher says, "Who the fuck _are_ you? Babe Ruth?"

Naz expects a slider but gets instead an arc curveball. Here it comes, nice and slow and perfectly crosses the plate thigh high on Naz. And as he swings, he utters, "Yuh," with a smile. "The Babe!"

He looks down at the catcher as he begins his four-bagger jog and says, "Yeah, dude, I'm Babe Ruth." And he laughs taking off trotting the bases. Boston holds New York down in the ninth, three up and three down. Naz stands up in front of the dugout waving his hat for all the fans applauding and screaming, whistling and calling his name.

There is cardboard, packing material and pamphlets of directions all over the tall skinny man's floor. He barely looks at the directions, since he's already got the knowledge stored up in his head. The rifle is incredibly tough but light too. He's got a tripod just under the end of the barrel, below the site. He is completely impressed with the stability. When he lays it down, there is no wobble, and when he holds it up to his shoulder, it is comfortable.

He has it broken down into four pieces and placed into four cut compartments in the cue case. By this time, he never gets frisked anymore. He knows everyone: Everyone knows him. But, he takes no chances.

It's the fifth game of five. The Yankees win two and the Red Sox two. If Boston takes tonight, they move up to 1st place in the Division. Sammy isn't scheduled to start. Pulling and trading is a surprise to everyone. He's pitched two full in the past four days, so he is required to rest. He has several pitching slots open but not enough to start. He plans to sit in the bull pen and cheer his team on. Just like the guy in the right field bleachers.

Cruza comes out to start the game. Besides Sammy, Cruza throws the nastiest pitches and has the longest repertoire. His issue is that he likes to show off his hundred-mile-an-hour Fastball. Sure, it's fast but none of them move enough to trick the batter. He gets hit a lot and dinged a lot. Skipper discerns that New York is weak on Fastballs, so he puts Cruza in anyway.

The first three innings are scoreless, but the Boston fielders are busier than they've been yet. Boston is hitting but not solid and nothing past the infield. In the top of the fourth, New York scores 2 runs on base hits. And then, like an echo, Boston comes up, and with two outs, gets two men on and Jimmy comes through with a deep two-bagger into the right field corner. He knocks in two runs but then he is left stranded.

The fifth and sixth innings are scoreless. In the top of the 7th, the lead-off man hits one out; a solo homerun that puts the Yankees one up. Three outs follow. Boston is at bat starting at the top of the order. This sequence of hits could not have been played out in a practice book of perfection. The first hit is a double high off the Green Monster. The second hit is a lobbed single to right-center, and the second-base runner makes it to third. Next in the lineup hits a line drive double, driving in another two runs. Once again, though, Boston leaves a man stranded.

Sitting crossed-legged in front of his seat, the bleacher cleaner is cool and calm. He has his non-metallic rifle pieced together. It's tight. It's solid. He looks to the ammo. He nearly completed this task at home last night, capping his own using ceramics, plastics, copper and aluminum high velocity materials, and calibrates his scope. Round-nosed ammunition will work well. One hunter he read about shot and killed a moose with a .22 rifle in Alaska. He read the book and watched the movie "Into the Wild," which talks about this. Neither offer anything to his application.

He lays down with his legs and feet underneath his seat. He has perfect posture for aiming at and shooting his target. Art is in his skybox and is in the crosshairs. The shooter owns a perfect posture. With Art in his sights, he rests a finger on the trigger and is ready to take his shot, but then, in a split-second decision, he hears the voice inside say something.

"If I kill Mr. Costello, he does not suffer: He just dies."

He's got a bead on the young little shitter, and he holds it and follows it with every movement. The lineup goes one, two, three, and Boston takes long strands off the field into the dugout.

There's no action in the bottom of the eighth but Boston is in the lead. All they must do is keep the Yankees down in the ninth. Sammy takes to the mound. The crowd goes dub-nuts. The translucent bead is once again on target, like a bullseye. The first batter goes down on a Gyroball, a Knuckle-Curve and a Cutter. A perfect sequence.

The second batter steps in and cocks his bat, and stares into the eyes of Sammy

Costello. He holds his bat belt high over the middle of the plate. The wind up delivers a slider, swung on and missed but there is a sound of a bat hitting a ball. And then, another sharp-sounding pop explodes in the stadium.

Jimmy runs out to the mound where Sammy is laying down. Trainers, paramedics, team physicians surround Sammy and ask everyone else to please step away.

"We've got an emergency on our hands!"

With everything in the case hastily wiped down and oiled, the tall, skinny man throws the case as hard as he can over the wall. He hopes that the case wedges between two vertical segments on the outside of Fenway. He then runs to his manager's office for orders. He is stopped three times on the way and briefly interrogated by the law.

"I work here as a maintenance man and a bleacher cleaner; right up there." He points at the right field nose bleed section.

He continues to the manager's office, where his boss tells him to find a seat: "We're all on lock down."

The left side of Sammy's head is bleeding. Art rushes down to the mound. People want to run, just run away. Meanwhile, security police and extra cops radioed in are trying to lock down the stadium. The attendees behind his observation booth have all run; to where, who knows?

With medics, Jimmy and Art surrounding him, Sammy sits up leaning back on his elbows.

"What the fuck happened this time? He missed the fucking ball!"

"Sammy, slow down. You've been shot in the head. What do you feel?"

"I feel like something hit me pretty hard right here in the middle side of my head. I've got a bad sudden, sharp headache."

The ambulance pulls away carrying Sammy and his father.

"Sammy, Sammy," Art pleads. "Talk to me. Please say something to your Dad."

The Paramedic suggests holding the young man's hand.

"Is he still alive?" Art cries.

"He is conscious at this point, sir. We'll be at Beth Israel Deaconess Medical Center in three minutes. Hold on now."

Sammy is immediately attended to. It is obviously one of two, or both rounds that hit Sammy in the head, bringing him down. As the surgeons operate, they keep a close eye on the pulse. It's no time for hospital police work just yet but they do have the weapon's trajectory. They radio-in to the Lieutenant stationed at Fenway.

The Press pick up on it and, of course, speculate; more imagination inflation.

"We're extremely sad to report the assassination of young Baseball phenomenon, Sammy Costello, of the Boston Red Sox. More as we get it."

CSI is all over the right field bleachers. They see nothing but garbage and trash all over.

"Jeez," one cop says. "The cleaning crew can't be an easy job."

"Yeah. . .Naw. . .Shit."

"Hey," one of the investigators gets everyone's attention. "What the fuck is this?"

He is clanging his nightstick across bars made to keep whoever is in there safe, and he says so.

"Hey Stump!" His boss calls him over. He is the smallest guy on the team.

"Yeah?"

"I want you to find the way in, and *carefully* perform a CSI. There'll always be someone nearby. Just call out if you need help or have retrieved an artifact."

"OK, boss. You got it."

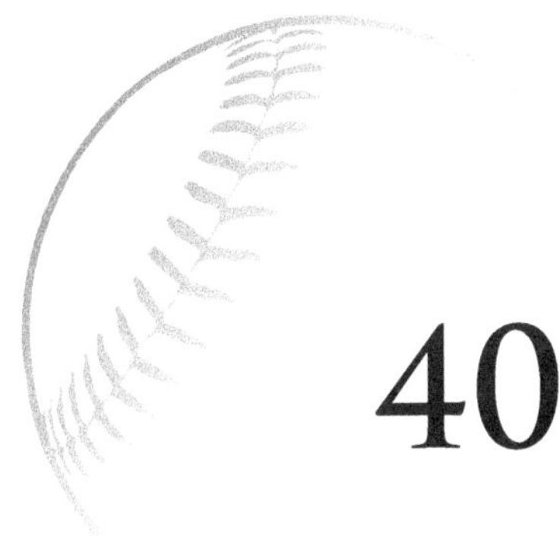

40

Very few leave the Park without a stop, frisk and interview. Women scream, they beg, and men begin to fight. The Boston Police Department have approximately 2,015 officers and 808 civilian personnel, with patrol services covering an area over 89 miles. Nearly one-quarter of the entire force is called out to Fenway.

Everyone's IDs are scanned while being questioned and while a detective team of 48 interrogate the entire Park Crew and staff. Stump orders sample tape to lift all the debris, and a fingerprint kit. According to the portable lab, he has at least three samples of foreign matter; black powder, ceramics and plastic.

Stump crawls back out of the caged seat and stands up, stretches and places his equipment hard-shell carrier and evidence bags down. He calls his Captain, who asks him to work closely with a small team that are on the way up. They are to look everywhere in the vicinity, leaving nothing to assumption.

"Holy shit, Stump. Look at this!"

"Well, we *are* up in the highest bleachers, brother."

"And this vertical alleyway. Look down there."

"It's all part of the original, old architecture. These verticals encircle three sides of Fenway Park."

"Well, to me," the detective begins. "These

verticals are an extension of our crime scene."

"OK. Done. Get a spot up here!" Stump commands.

In between the two columns directly behind the attendant's cage, they see something. It's pitch black down there, so even with the spot light, the object is unidentifiable.

"Lieutenant, we see something, sir."

"Well, what the Christ is it?"

"We can't tell from up here. Get someone with a high-powered search light to look between the two columns we've got the spot on. We're directly over the right field bleachers."

The detectives on the ground use a ladder to peak over the 12-foot divider between the two columns. They move the light no more than six inches at a time to get a look at all the crap in the crevasse.

"We've got a hit! We've got something!"

They set up a pully and drop a man down there to retrieve the object. He brings out what looks like a pool cue case, and a nice one at that. A lead CSI investigator gloves up, opens the case and finds a handsome as hell custom stick.

The molded interior appears to be loose. CSI on the ground gently lifts the sculpt and hands it over to his partner.

"Well, gwawd-dammut would you look at that! A fucking plastic rifle? Cheezes!"

"Get me a metallic scanner."

"Not one positive ping, boss."

"Get this and Stump's evidence bag to the Lab, ASAP!"

They've got prints all over the place. They are sure who they belong to, as they have an indisputable match. The suspect remains nameless but is kept in custody under observation.

In the wee hours of Monday morning, the BPD conduct a raid on the subject's apartment. He doesn't have much, but the police do collect cardboard boxes and dividers, plastic blasting caps, black powder, ceramics and assorted tools. Finally, they carry out his laptop.

There is a match on the ceramic, black powder and plastic between what is found in the stadium and the apartment. One of the last Interweb Bookmarks and Historic entries on his laptop are underground weapons sites. It's kind of like Silk Road for firearms.

Witnesses from the Fenway Park employee pool testify freely that the case came in and out of the Park nearly every day. It passes the security checks, including that for metallic material. The story is that the guy is an avid pool enthusiast always looking for someone to shoot with him.

"Yeah. . .*Shoot*."

"But all that could be a front to set security at ease and suspicions down low."

"And he passes that check with ease when he finally fits his rifle into the forged construct below the stick and enters Fenway."

The suspect is held at Logan Airport, Boston, as he attempts to board a flight for the Mediterranean. He is taken into custody and interrogated thoroughly. He is presented with reams of affidavits and testimony that he's asked to speak to.

"Mister Art Costello, please. This is Detective John Radmonelli from the BPD."

Sophia asks him to hold for a moment.

"Hello. This is Art Costello." There is absolutely no inflection in his voice. It's monotone and tired.

"Detective John Radmonelli from the BPD."

"Yes?"

"I have a couple questions for you, if you wouldn't mind."

"Sure. Go ahead."

"Do you know of anyone that would want to hurt Sammy, or you, or anyone else in your family?"

"Let me see. Nobody should hate me that much, God forbid."

"Are you familiar with a man named Hubert Bobotonis?"

"Jesus. Naw, I don't think. . ." Art begins. "Wait! Yes! He is my ex-son-in-law! We use a nickname 'Bo' to snip the syllables but that is him, for sure."

"I am very sorry, Mister Costello. He is the individual who shot your son."

"He is my daughter -- with child -- Anita's ex-husband."

"He fully admits there is animosity among you all; Perhaps others in your family."

"Besides the obvious, who would be my young daughter Anita, I'm the only one in the family who has stepped up and done anything about him and his terrible behavior in times past."

"Most men would stand by their children, sir."

"What is he charged with?"

"We are holding him right now but when we get the results from the Hospital or Coroner, the worst case would be Capital Murder, 1st Degree.”

“So, he’d be up for execution. . .”

“Mister Costello, please allow me to read and address the subject. Capital punishment is a legal penalty in the U.S. state of New Hampshire. The only crime punishable by it is capital murder. Listen:

“Since 1734, twenty-four people have been executed, with the last execution carried out in 1939. As of 1976, there is only one condemned man in the state, and no execution facility. New Hampshire is the lone remaining state in New England allowing capital punishment.

“Lethal injection is currently the primary legal form of execution, though hanging can be utilized if lethal injection is determined to be ‘impractical to carry out the punishment of death.' Between 1868 and 1939, executions took place at the New Hampshire State Prison for Men in Concord. The long hiatus on executions means that while officially considered a 'retentionist' state, only four US states have *not* performed executions more recently than New Hampshire: Maine, Minnesota, North Dakota, and Wisconsin. And only two countries in the European Union Sweden and Portugal." The detective comes to a rest.

"I'm just going to say it: He's guilty in the courtroom. I mean, come on. And the crime was committed in Massachusetts." Art is all nerved up.

"Mister Costello, Bobotonis has offered his confession for a life sentence, thus excluding Capital Punishment; the death penalty, and Parole."

"Detective, I have a question."

"Yes, Mr. Costello?"

"Why Sammy? Why would he want to hurt Sammy?"

"The suspect testifies that his original plan was to kill *you. . .YOU. . .*but then, he changed his mind."

"Changed his mind? Changed his mind? What the fuck is going on Detective?"

"Killing you wouldn't hurt you, sir. You would not suffer. But killing Sammy would have you suffer for the rest of your life. I'm sorry sir, but those are his words."

Everybody in the Costello family continue to pace and wander around the first-floor hospital halls and corridors with mind-body disconnect. They don't know what to think or what to do.

Finally, Art explains the case to them but tells them if they fight in court, it will drag up every worm out of any dirt found on them; out of them.

"This would obviously be toughest on Anita. On those grounds, I say, *"Let him rot in a cage!"*

"As for most of my parts in all of this, of which none of you are aware, they would also be brought to light. And I, personally, and for the sake of this family, do not want my intimate business records and affairs exposed," Art says.

An ER doctor approaches. "The left side of Sammy's head would have been blown off."

"Would have? So, yeah? What now?"

"The titanium plate in Sammy's head saved him; saved his life. We are picking out very small bits of ceramic and plastic from the flesh over and around the metal plate."

"What the heck does that mean?"

"Let me send a CSI investigator to explain things to you."

"Mr. Costello," the police inspector greets Art. "We may have witnessed a miracle today."

"How so, sir?"

"The weapon used is a non-metallic kit gun; a rifle. But what is key here is that the ammunition is hand-made, like the rifle is, in the suspect's home. He finished it at his workstation at the Park. That ammo is made solely with a synthetic casing and a bullet of compressed ceramic sediment and plastic."

"What the huh? I've never heard of such a thing!"

"We haven't either up close, although we are aware of their existence. Those two rounds would have easily killed any other man. No doubt. But the matter and velocity were no match for the titanium head plate.

"Everything really does happen for a reason. Oh, my God, I have to sit down."

While Bo sits quietly, legs Indian-crossed, and blindingly stares at the steel door of a 10-foot cell, Sammy is sitting up in bed eating ice cream and carrying on with his euphoric family and the ER attendants.

THE END

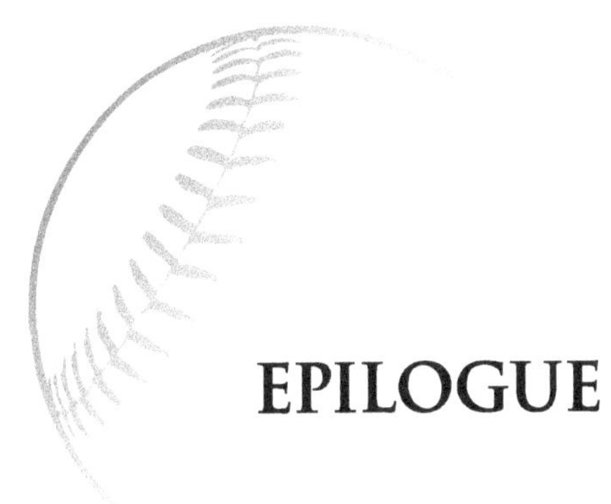

EPILOGUE

Hubert Bobotonis is sentenced to 75 years. He is up for parole in 45 years. He joins the Prison Vocational Foods Club and continues doing what he does best: flipping and cooking.

Sammy Costello returns to action within two weeks and continues to pitch record seasons with the Boston Red Sox. He invents a pitch after a few years back in action. It is called a "Riser." It approaches the plate seemingly sinking fast. Then, at the last moment, it rises sharply into his target; typically, the knees. The grip is the first two fingers, riding on the two inside seams, cradling his thumb at the bottom and with his smallest fingers tucked in under the right bottom of the ball.

Just another unhittable Sammy pitch.

Credits

--[1] -- Baseball America© | Scouts on Scouts

Partial Content Used with Permission

--Cover Photo--

Basis of Cover Art Image

Portions used with permission via the TheBaseballZone©

Editors include the author, his personal editor and the publisher's editing team.

www.ingramcontent.com/pod-product-compliance
Lightning Source LLC
Chambersburg PA
CBHW060755210726
48292CB00013B/150